Have Yourself a Billionaire for Christmas

TRACEY LIVESAY

Copyright © 2023 by Tracey Livesay

All rights reserved.

This is a work of fiction. Names, characters, places, and incidents are products of the author's imagination or are used fictitiously and are not to be construed as real. Any resemblance to actual events, locales, organizations, or persons, living or dead, is entirely coincidental.

No part of this book may be used or reproduced in any manner whatsoever without written permission except in the case of brief quotations embodied in critical articles and reviews.

Cover by Natasha Snow

Edited by Rochelle French

Excerpt from *American Royalty* copyright © 2022 by Tracey Livesay

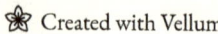 Created with Vellum

To the man who continues to give me pleasure...

Prologue

The Grinches Who Stole Corporate Philanthropy
www.livingthrugiving.com

It's that time of the year where we get to judge who's been naughty and who's been nice.

Overall, corporate giving is around eighteen billion dollars, which sounds impressive. But as a percentage of pre-tax earnings, that number is really a shameful amount, especially when you consider corporate giving hasn't kept pace with the sharp increase in executive salaries. On average, top corporations (those on the Fortune 100 list) give forty percent less than the amount given by average-size corporations. And that doesn't seem fair.

Shame on you, CEOs!

Below we list the Top Five companies destined to find a lump of coal in their stockings this holiday season.

#1. Berl Lumber & Hardware. With its impressive twenty billion in revenue and four billion in profits, this go-to home improvement store sponsors two professional auto racing teams and a college football bowl game, and yet has no named or registered philanthropic program. Do we really want this company to help us renovate our homes when their own corporate house leaves a lot to be desired?

#2. Organic Grown Grocery. Customers shop OGG, especially on Seven Percent Sundays, because they believe doing so helps the company's many philanthropic efforts. Would they still be willing to pay premium prices for average goods if they knew the multibillion-dollar company's promise to match up to two million dollars—which sounds like a lot—accounts for only .008 percent of their total net profits?

#3. Rand Realty Group. The country's foremost developer of luxury shopping malls made two point seven billion dollars in revenue last year, but it donated less than twenty million dollars to charity. Hey RRG, instead of opening a new town center in the next mid-major metropolis, how about investing those dollars to help that city's poor and low-income populations?

Chapter One

Five days until Christmas

F As Jackson Randolph IV limped from the windblown entryway into the great room, irritation tightened his chest and beads of perspiration bloomed from his skin to dot his brow and upper lip. His injured knee throbbed, his head ached, and the only incentive strong enough to make bearable the fifteen-hour journey from London to Wyoming had been the thought of the luxuriously plush king-sized bed in the guest room of his sister's spacious but private ski chalet.

A bed he'd already be in if not for the light from the sixty-five-inch flat screen TV mounted above the fireplace that had detoured him in this direction. He had no doubt the housekeeper had left it on, usually a negligible offense. However, since every unnecessary action caused him immense pain, he was finding it difficult to be charitable.

"...*who's been naughty and who's been nice in the corporate world*..."

Jackson's gaze flew to the screen, its low volume barely audible.

Speaking of charitable...

It seemed the universe was seeking ways to fuck with him.

The chyron beneath the entertainment news talking head read: Top Five Grinches in Corporate America.

Son of a bitch!

He clenched his teeth so hard that he knew he'd be able to add jaw pain to all the others. In the weeks since that fucking Living Thru Giving article had gone viral, he hadn't been able to escape it.

"Third on the list is Jackson Randolph and Rand Realty Group. Mr. Randolph can't be bothered to give to charity, but the handsome CEO can apparently be called a giver in other ways. Will he spend the holidays giving something very nice to one lucky lady?"

A picture flashed on the screen showing him climbing the steps of the RRG corporate plane behind an attractive woman.

Absolute nonsense! He wasn't jet-setting around the world like some shallow playboy. He was conducting business, which he did twenty-four seven. In fact, the woman boarding the plane was his very happily married CFO.

Jackson spied the remote control on the wood and stone coffee table situated in front of the large sectional sofa, and after several more agonizing steps, he grabbed it and turned the TV off. The action plunged the room into darkness, save for the moonlight pouring in through the enormous great room windows.

Exhaling, he sank onto the arm of the couch and massaged his sore knee. The injury had happened a week ago when he'd tried to evade the press outside his office building—one more debacle that fucking article was responsible for. Quietly, he muttered to himself, "I do *not* have time for this."

"Oh, my god!"

The unexpected female shriek sent his heart from his chest to his throat. He jumped up—bad move—and turned to see a figure on the couch bolt upright and send a blanket sailing through the air. Long, slender legs flailed, and a foot caught his thigh above the site of his recent injury.

He saw stars. Literally.

Pain radiated down his quad and he groaned, stumbling back. Frantic, unintelligible noises emanated from the woman as she scrambled away from him, pushing a mass of dark brown and amber curls from her face, and—

Those curls...

His narrowed eyes now adjusted to the dim lighting and—

Holy shit! It couldn't be *her*. How could *she* be *here*?

But there was no mistaking the identity of the woman staring wide-eyed at him.

Rachel Williams was just as beautiful as he'd remembered, with gorgeous features that had wrenched the air from his lungs the first time he laid eyes on her, six months ago. He'd dreamed of her and those amazing ringlets, recalled clasping one and watching it capture his finger snugly, the same way her pussy would hold that same finger later on that evening...

"For God's sake, calm down," he ordered, holding his palms up, facing outward. "It's me, Jackson. I'm not going to hurt you."

Rachel's mouth snapped shut and she sagged back against a huge throw pillow. "Jack?" Her voice was still low and raspy from sleep, but the terror from a moment ago appeared to have receded. She reached over and switched on the side table lamp, flooding the room in a golden halo of light. "What are you doing here?"

His back stiffened. "I could ask you the same thing." He glanced about, taking in the place. He hadn't been here since before his sister renovated. Joss had done a great job, and now the chic, rustic interior could've been featured on the front page of any design website.

"You could, but I asked you first. And since you were the one who barged in on me—"

"I did not barge—" Jackson broke off, too exhausted to engage in what he recognized as the opening bars of an argument. That was the other thing he remembered about Rachel. She possessed an uncanny ability to frustrate him more than any other woman he'd ever met.

Both literally and figuratively.

In fact, the only time they hadn't argued after meeting was when their tongues had been otherwise occupied.

With each other's.

He cleared his throat. "I needed to get away for a few days."

"Uh-huh. Nice try, Scrooge McJack," she said, swinging her black legging-clad legs around and resting bare feet on the area rug covering the wide plank wooden floor. "I saw the article online. And on TV."

"Fuck." He shoved a hand through his hair.

She pursed her lips. "Not with me. You had more important things to do. Remember?"

He would never live that incident down, but he'd add it to the growing list of misconceptions about him. Along with the idea that he was the modern-day version of some Victorian holiday miser. He couldn't believe the major outlets had picked up an article by a small online financial magazine. And he definitely couldn't believe said article was about to ruin everything he'd spent the past seven years trying to rebuild.

His left knee twinged, and despite his attempt at stoicism, he winced.

"Are you okay?" Rachel asked, ridges appearing between her brows as she stared up at him. "You look odd."

But she looked amazing. He'd already glimpsed those long legs he'd hungered for, and now he was having a hard time averting his gaze from the silhouette of her soft breasts, visible beneath her long sleeve white T-shirt—emblazoned with *Every Day is Earth Day*. He finally managed to raise his gaze...only to meet her luminescent eyes. Whiskey-colored and thickly lashed, they tilted slightly at the corners.

Those eyes.

In the darkened coat check room in that DC hotel, with his fingers inside of her, her eyes had practically glowed when she'd come in his arms.

"Is that your polite way of saying I look like shit?" He'd seen himself in his plane's bathroom mirror before he disembarked.

His brown hair stood in spikes from forehead to crown and the dark circles highlighting his bloodshot eyes and stubble-covered cheeks would've had most people steering clear of him. The long day had started early that morning, several time zones over, when his sister first called him with the brilliant idea to stay in her chalet while the intense scrutiny from the article blew over.

"Of course not," Rachel said quickly. Her lashes flickered and she bit her lip. "It's freezing outside, but you're sweating."

Her instantaneous response and the vulnerability it exposed intrigued him, but his knee spasmed and he recognized the warning for what it was: a prelude to his fortitude deserting him. He barely had time to twist his body—to avoid falling face first—before he collapsed next to her on the couch.

She gasped and held out her hand before letting it fall. "Jack! Are you okay?"

Oh yeah, she'd loved shortening his name, particularly after he told her it annoyed him. Unlike his sister, he'd never wanted a nickname.

The cushions next to him dipped but he ignored the movement, instead leaning his head back and closing his eyes, focusing on breathing in and out. Shit. How could his knee hurt this much? He hadn't torn his ACL or ripped any tendons. He'd only twisted it. Unfortunately, his patella hadn't gotten the pain differential memo.

He'd followed the doctor's orders to rest, ice, and elevate it… mostly. Okay, he had done so a few times, but he couldn't sit around doing nothing. He ran a multi-billion-dollar corporation that held meetings all over the world. Traveling was an essential part of his business.

Which was where the pills his doctor had prescribed for pain management came into play. But he refused to rely on narcotics, needing to be clear-headed and in control of his faculties, even if it meant dealing with a little discomfort.

"Jack?"

He flinched, then sighed at the feel of a cool cloth on his forehead. He inhaled, and a familiar scent, one he'd dubbed "sexy citrus," teased him.

"What happened to you?" Rachel asked.

He refused to look at her. "It's not a big deal. I'll be fine. I just need a second."

The silence was thick with her disapproval. Then came her terse, "Suit yourself."

This time when the cushion next to him shifted, he opened his eyes to see her standing in front of him, stretching. The action elongated her torso and allowed him a quick glimpse of the bared honey beige skin above her waistband, but when she noticed his stare, she stopped and let her arms fall to her sides.

A pity.

Pain pulsed in his knee and bonded with the growing bruise on his thigh, driving his attention away from Rachel and back to where it belonged—on his injury. He smoothed his palm over the area in a futile attempt to lessen the ache.

She glanced at his leg. Frowned. "Are you traveling by yourself?"

"What?"

Her brows drew together. "Is there someone who came with you? Someone who can help?"

"I don't need help," he countered.

"The waxy pallor of your skin, the way you're kneading your thigh, your face plant... It doesn't take Nancy Drew to unravel the clues. You're injured, and I'm concerned."

For some reason, her concern pissed him off. "I appreciate your interest, but it isn't necessary."

"Fine. Then I'll ask you again—and no bullshit, please—what are you doing here?"

He swiped a hand over his face. Rachel had been tenacious during their prior conversation, too, unwilling to let any point of disagreement go until they'd discussed it to death and she'd tried her absolute best to change his mind. If he didn't give her a suitable response, she'd be on him all night. And not in the fun way.

As if he was in any condition to have "fun" with Rachel.

"I was in London," he said, "but the press was staking out my office and I didn't want to deal with them. I need to be in Portland before the twenty-third, and I wanted a place to lie low. Wyoming is a lot closer to Oregon than DC is, so it made sense to come here instead of going home."

Rachel crossed her arms over her chest. "The twenty-third? That's three days away."

"I know."

"Your client actually agreed to meet you the day before Christmas Eve instead of spending that time with their family or friends?"

His jaw tightened in irritation at her question. Not really, but she didn't need to know that. "In business, people tend to accommodate me. I'm kind of a big deal."

"In your own mind."

He narrowed his eyes. "That's not what you moaned in my ear when you confirmed my size for yourself."

Her eyes widened. "You're not a gentleman for bringing that up," she said snippily, her slight southern accent becoming more pronounced.

What the hell, Jackson? Why would you say that? Still— "I never said I was a gentleman."

"True. That assumption was my mistake, never to be repeated." She cleared her throat. "So you needed to get away. How did you end up at *this* house?"

"My sister owns it."

Her head jerked back. "You're kidding."

"No. Why?"

"Because my boss's friend owns this house, and I was told I could stay here. That it would have—" she air-quoted "—everything I needed during the holidays."

He frowned. What was Joss playing at, lending her house out when she told him he could use it? Did she know Rachel would be there? He dismissed the thought—he'd never spoken to Joss about his encounter with Rachel.

"You traveled across the country to spend the holidays alone in a stranger's house?" he asked, squinting up at her. "That makes no sense."

"And how is the sense of my actions any of *your* concern?"

He opened his mouth to respond, then closed it. She was right. It wasn't any of his business.

She wasn't his business.

And if she had his sister's permission, her presence here wasn't any of his business, either. He just wished if that were the case, Joss would have shared that important piece of information with him before he'd flown all the way here.

This entire conversation only confirmed that he and Rachel Williams were better off keeping any interaction between them at an impersonal level. Though he'd been angry when she'd ditched him back in June, he'd probably dodged a bullet. He didn't want or need that kind of distraction in his life. He'd be leaving in three days. The chalet was large enough that they could keep their distance, and with a full-time staff, they would never be alone.

Speaking of...

"What time does Amy arrive in the morning?" Jackson asked.

"Who?"

"Amy. The housekeeper," he explained when her brows remained linked in the middle of her forehead.

"Oh!" Rachel's expression cleared. She waved a slender hand. "You mean Amelia. I gave her the holiday off."

She did *what?* Jackson felt his blood pressure rising. "You didn't have the right to do that."

"I was the only one here." Rachel shrugged. "Her mother was feeling ill, and I don't need a housekeeper. The place was already well stocked, so I told her to go be with her mom and enjoy the holiday with her family."

He closed his eyes and pinched the bridge of his nose. The woman was a walking bleeding heart, willing to lend assistance or risk life and limb to help any living creature she deemed in peril. Which was great for Amy—*Amelia*—but extremely inconvenient for him. He'd anticipated having staff on hand who could tend to whatever he needed as his knee healed. Cook, clean, haul in firewoo—

He repressed the yawn yearning to break free. It would be smart to deal with this now, but the exhaustion that had been held at bay by finding her here was now catching up to him. He'd have to figure out his next move in the morning.

Bracing a hand on the arm of the sofa, he started to stand, but his knee immediately locked up, guaranteeing it wouldn't hold his weight. He fell back onto the cushion.

She leaned toward him. "Still insisting you don't need help?"

Dammit! Could he appear even more weak and feeble in front of this woman?

He shook his head. "I'm fine."

She jerked her chin upward. "Then stand up."

"No, I'm good."

She laughed. "You're such a baby."

He didn't know why he was acting this way. Maybe the injury and the long travel had affected his usual comportment? He made the mistake of looking at her, and the radiance of her smile reached into his chest and scorched his heart.

And her?

"Here." She grabbed his hand, anchored herself against the sofa, and pulled.

He—underestimating her strength because of her slender frame—put the considerable heft of his six-three, one-ninety build into rising.

She—probably thinking he was unable to help—tugged with surprising power.

The result had them teetering precariously until he overcorrected on his stable leg and then they were suddenly standing toe to toe, hip to hip, and he was gazing down at her upturned face.

"Thank you," she breathed, clutching his biceps tightly, her touch warm even through the layers of his clothing.

Blood abandoned every part of his body and rushed straight to his dick, as if heeding an inaudible call.

God, she smelled amazing, like sugared citrus, warm spices, and some indefinable scent that made his mouth water. This close he could see the dark striations of her irises that flared from the dilated pupils in her beautiful light brown eyes, could feel the plush softness of her breasts where they pressed against his chest, could hear the audible catch in her breathing before it quickened.

He swallowed, and his heart pounded as if it wished to leave a permanent impression against the wall of his chest. His hands flexed where they rested on her hips, his fingers curling to graze the top of her tight, round ass.

He'd experienced this immediate attraction the first time he met her. It had been so strong that he'd felt powerless against the seductive haze that had threatened to overwhelm him. Even now, knowing what he did and taking into account what he'd just promised himself, he was willing to throw caution to the wind for another taste of her.

A becoming rose color tinted her round cheekbones and she exhaled, drawing his attention to her mouth. A flash of pink appeared as her tongue darted out to moisten her bottom lip. He moved closer, even as he waged an internal battle to resist the instinct to dip his head and re-introduce her tongue to his.

What the hell are you doing?

He wished he knew. He inched a step back, wobbled, and her hand slid from his arm to grab his elbow. A surge of electricity skipped across his skin in the wake of her touch.

Yeah, this wasn't going to work.

He pulled away from her, steadied himself, and moved slowly from the sofa. "If you'll excuse me, I've been traveling for a long time and I'm exhausted. I'm going to bed now. In the morning, we'll see about getting you other accommodations."

"Other accommodations?" she asked with an edge to her tone as she shoved her hands on her hips.

He shifted his gaze away, her lovely, tempting image the one thing that might convince him to change his mind. "We can't both stay in this chalet."

"I was here first. If you don't like having me around, *you* leave. Or you can stay, and we can ignore each other. It's a huge house. Shouldn't be a problem."

There were plenty of reasons the two of them staying in the house would be a problem, starting with the countless number of things he wanted to do to her sexy mouth. Things he had to avoid at all costs. He narrowed his eyes. "Do you seriously think we could stay here together? Alone?"

She pursed those incredible lips. "I hate to break it to you, but you're not irresistible."

"Really? The first and only time we ever met, we almost fucked in the coat check room at an event attended by three hundred people. If that doesn't make me irresistible, what does it make you?"

Her expression shifted. Tightened. Irritation morphed into disgust, which scorched his skin. "It makes *you* an asshole. And you're right. Four thousand square feet *isn't* big enough for the both of us. I'll call my boss in the morning and make other arrangements."

She stalked across the great room and out of sight. A door slammed.

Jackson worked his jaw and forced himself to disregard the hard knot forming in his gut. Not his finest hour, by a long shot. No one would ever accuse him of being a saint, but he usually didn't go out of his way to be a prick. Rachel's lack of control wasn't at issue; it was his own.

Because despite his emotional churning at returning to the cloakroom and finding her gone, despite his anger at her insistence on ignoring him, despite his determination to forget she even existed, seeing her again reminded him that when it came to

Rachel Williams, *he* was at the mercy of his hormones instead of his brain. One crook of her finger and he'd risk those harmful emotions to be with her again.

With exhaustion once again tugging on his consciousness, he limped toward his room, cursing himself for not taking the crutch the doctor had offered him. The first of many dreadful decisions, culminating in his contemptible remark to Rachel. He owed her an apology. But first, he'd get some much-needed rest and hope that would prevent him from acting like a bastard during their next encounter.

The house contained a split floor plan, and he headed toward the cluster of bedrooms on the right, forcing himself not to look toward the corridor that led to the master. When he reached the room at the end of the hallway, he opened the door and stopped short at the sight of the curvaceous rear end bent over an open suitcase on the bench at the foot of the bed. His settled cock roused to attention.

"This is my room." He said the first thing he could think of, which again made him sound infantile. He blamed it on his southward-bound blood.

Rachel slowly straightened and turned to face him. "I was told I could use any room I wanted. I chose this one because the biggest room is on the other side of the house. That room, I'd assumed, was the master."

"It is." He shoved a hand in his pocket, pressed his erection against his leg to neutralize it and hoped she'd misunderstand the reasoning behind the casual-looking gesture. "But this one has the view of the mountains."

"I know." A furrow crinkled the smoothness of her brow. "That's why I picked it."

"Fine." The word emerged rough from his clenched jaw.

So much for not acting like a bastard during their next encounter.

He withdrew, shutting the door behind him, and headed back over to the master, but when he reached the second guest bedroom several feet later, he surrendered to his body's demand and went inside, diving for the bed before his knee could dump him on the ground. He rolled to his back and relaxed onto the pillow-topped queen mattress, closing his eyes.

He'd overdone it. Both Joss and his doctor would have something to say about that.

"This isn't the master," Rachel said from the doorway.

"I'm aware. But it'll do for now. I've got my—fuck. My bag." His lids popped open and he sat up, gesturing wearily. "I left it by the front door."

He tried to stand but his knee objected. Vigorously.

She rolled her eyes. "I'll get it."

A couple of minutes later she returned, holding his leather duffel.

"Thank you," he said, never having meant any words more.

"You're welcome. See, I helped you and it was nice, wasn't it? Your company should try it sometime. Helping others, that is." She dropped his bag on the bed and stalked out of the room.

Great. Everyone was a fucking critic. Or members of the philanthropy police.

As soon as he heard the door to her room close, he reached into his bag and pulled out the bottle of pills his doctor had prescribed for the pain. His leg burned as if he'd been stabbed with a red-hot fire poker and he knew if he didn't get some sleep, he'd be unable to function in the morning. A state of being that didn't bode well for him, as evidenced by his behavior this evening. He normally wasn't the asshole she'd called him, but pain, exhaustion, and seeing the woman who'd ghosted him had triggered all the worst parts of his personality. His cock still throbbed in response to seeing her again. It had been lust at first sight that night in June, and though he'd done his best to forget her, it was obvious that what he'd done hadn't worked.

All of which he could analyze at another time. He needed his mind, his leg, and his hard-on to ease so he could sleep. He shook two tablets into his palm, swallowed them dry, and settled back against the pillow.

Fifteen minutes later, the only pain that had eased was the one in his knee.

Dammit!

For the second time that evening, he admitted defeat. He gritted his teeth even as his hand drifted to the button of his pants. Rachel Williams had reduced him to little more than a horny teenager jerking himself off, unable to control his own body.

They both couldn't stay here, which meant, despite what he'd told her, he had to go.

Chapter Two

What a jackass! Rachel stormed back into her room and slammed the door.

A week ago, her boss had offered up this house to Rachel after an incident in DC required she immediately leave town for a brief period. Of all the people who could've walked in here, how did she end up with the serious misfortune of seeing that too-gorgeous-for-his-own-good Jackson Randolph again?

It had taken everything she had not to blush continually as she'd looked at him. The man's fingers had been inside of her, for Christ's sake!

But the longer she remained in his presence, the easier it got. He seemed to strike only two chords within her: anger and desire.

The desire was obvious. The first time she'd met him, she'd been bowled over by his thick brown hair, deep blue eyes, and angular, chiseled features. The black, tailored, slim cut suit he wore looked like it cost more than her rent and fit him impeccably.

The man who'd startled her awake wasn't as polished as her coatroom tryster. His brown hair was tousled, there was a reddish hue to the beard covering and yet he was still the sexiest man she'd ever seen.

The anger came from who he was and what he represented. What she'd found out *after* she'd almost given herself to him.

She'd attended a DC fundraiser for work and had met Jackson when she slipped out to the bar to take a break from all the glad-handing and kajillionaires patting themselves on the back for their charity.

He bought her a drink, and for the next hour they sparred over everything from philosophy to politics to the success of various DC sport franchises. And through it all, anticipation for something more sizzled between them, evident in the flush upon his cheekbones, his slow and intimate smiles, and the moisture pooling between her thighs.

When the chemistry grew too strong for either to ignore, he took her hand and tugged her down the hall. They found a dark, abandoned cloakroom. As soon as the door closed behind them, he pulled her close and claimed her lips in a kiss that threatened to mark her soul. She moaned, gripping his upper arms for stability as his hands roamed everywhere, eventually bringing her to orgasm.

She'd just leaned her forehead against his, trying to catch her breath, when his phone had beeped. A few seconds later, it beeped again. When it chirped for a third time, he'd cursed and checked his texts. Apologizing, he told her he had to take care of something, but promised he'd return quickly.

"Don't leave. Promise you'll wait for me."

He'd gazed into her eyes and left her with one thorough, back-arching kiss that had her determined to wait as long as was necessary.

Until, through the closing door, she heard someone greet him as Jackson Randolph and then praise him for his latest town center development.

Her excitement had withered on the vine and died.

To learn the man who'd intrigued her, who'd captured her

interest for the first time in years, who'd made her body hum and burn for his touch, had been another elite, money-hungry, power-grabbing businessman had left her feeling disillusioned and disappointed.

And stupid.

Why couldn't he have been someone else? A wish she'd repeated to herself many times since she'd left the cloakroom, her dignity in shatters, but her barriers re-built.

Rachel knew what she wanted, and Jackson Randolph wasn't it. She longed for what her parents had managed to have for the past thirty-five years: a sweet, gentle love affair, traveling the world, helping others in need. That required a tolerant, amiable type of man. A teacher, like her father. Not some rich asshole who'd been born on third base but thought he'd hit a triple.

A selfish jerk, in other words.

She wasn't the only one who thought of Jackson in that way. She'd read the recent article that had called out his company, Rand Realty Group, and their woeful corporate giving. That alone reinforced her belief that she'd made the right call to walk away from him that night. His company could be helping so many people, but they refused to contribute more than a negligible amount to charity, even given their annual revenue. Jackson and his executives and his shareholders had more money than they could spend in a lifetime. But for people like him, it wasn't enough. It would never be enough. They'd clutch onto every last dollar just to keep others from having it.

"See, I helped you and it was nice, wasn't it? Your company should try it sometime."

She pursed her lips. She probably should've kept that parting shot to herself. But did it make what she said any less true? Besides, she'd never been good at keeping her opinions to herself. One would think after twenty-seven years on this earth, she would've learned. But no, she was still leading with her chin and getting clocked for her troubles.

That didn't excuse the way she'd responded to Jackson. Just

because he'd acted like a douche didn't mean she had to stoop to his level. She needed to call Sharon and let her know about Jackson's arrival, but a quick glance at the clock on her nightstand showed it was too late back east to disturb her boss. She'd talk to her in the morning and offer her apologies; explain the situation and pre-empt Jackson before he went to his sister. Because Rachel knew that's what he would do. Men like him, used to getting what they wanted, always complained when they didn't.

He needs help. You saw him. He could barely stand.

Ha! Let his ego help him stand! She wouldn't stay anywhere she wasn't welcome. Plus, the situation had probably cleared up back in DC. She'd been here a week, long enough for things to have been resolved. The house was nice, and she appreciated the gesture, but lounging in a ski chalet simply wasn't her.

It was time for her to go back home, back to where she belonged.

Four days until Christmas

"What do you mean, I can't come home?" Rachel asked, frustration tightening her chest as she stared at her boss's worried image on her iPad the next morning.

Years ago, Rachel had taken a job at the Turner Foundation, an organization focused on the education of women throughout the world. Her belief in the Foundation's mission and her passion for her work had brought her to the attention of Sharon Gilmore, the CEO, who'd promoted Rachel to her Executive Assistant, a job she'd held for the past two years. It was Sharon she'd turned to when she'd needed help.

Sharon bit her lower lip and tucked the strands of her sleek black bob behind one ear. "The police said they'd received several reports of the guy skulking about in front of your apartment building yesterday."

Shit.

Rachel glanced away from the screen to the winter wonderland out her bedroom window. She'd awakened to the ground covered with snow as far as the eye could see, the horizon blending into the majestic snow-capped mountains. A world away from the chaos she'd left behind.

Her stomach churned and she fumbled with the tiny gold stud in her right earlobe. "Did he cause a commotion, or bother any of the other tenants?"

"He didn't go inside. Several people called 911 when he was there for more than ten minutes because they didn't like the looks of him." Sharon paused. "A couple of them swore he had a gun."

What the hell? The man who was stalking her had a *gun?*

Rachel clenched her hands into fists to keep them from trembling. "Why didn't the police call me?"

Sharon's features softened in understanding. "I'm sure they will. But with my connections in the city and Greg's ties to the mayor's office, they agreed to our request to be kept in the loop."

This was all Rachel's fault. Because she couldn't help from stepping in when she saw someone in need.

Three weeks ago, she'd been walking home from the metro late at night when she noticed a couple having a heated discussion near the entrance of her apartment building. As someone who'd lived in the city for years she was used to dramatic public displays, but something about the man's bared teeth and sweeping arm gestures and the woman's bulging eyes and cringing posture set off her alarm bells.

She slid her phone from her back pocket and slowed her steps, attempting to give herself more time to observe them without seeming obvious. The woman turned away, but the man grabbed her arm and spun her so violently that she nearly toppled forward.

Rachel went into savior mode. She hurried over to the couple. "Are you okay?" she asked the woman.

The man, wearing a dirty and ripped jacket, pulled the woman closer. "We're fine. Mind your fucking business!"

"I'm not talking to you. Are you okay?" Rachel again asked the young woman, who was visibly trembling.

The woman's eyes flickered from Rachel to the man and back again before she shook her head.

His pale face reddened, and he tightened his hold on the woman's arm until she cried out.

"Stop!" Rachel shouted. "I called 911 before I approached you. The police will be here soon. We don't need to have any trouble. Just walk away. Now."

The man stared at her, then yanked at the woman's arm one more time before he released it. "You better watch your back, bitch," he spat at Rachel. To the woman he said, "I'll be seeing you, Crystal."

Not taking her eyes off the man, Rachel held out her hand to Crystal. "Come on. We can wait for the police in my building."

A moment later, they were in Rachel's apartment's vestibule behind the locked front door...where she finally dialed 911.

Although Crystal had been able to identify the man to the police, he'd evaded capture. Based on his record, the police had been concerned about Rachel's safety. Initially, she hadn't taken the assumed threat seriously, but when she'd spied the guy two weeks later while on her way to work, panic had seized hold of her. She'd detoured, heading to the nearest public place where she ducked inside and called law enforcement.

They'd suggested she get away while they continued to search for the man. When Sharon heard what happened, she'd offered Rachel the use of the chalet in Wyoming. Rachel had arrived less than a day later.

"So, it looks like you'll need to stay there a little longer," Sharon said, her words bringing Rachel out of her reverie.

Crap.

What was she going to do? It was clear she couldn't go home yet. She might not like the idea of the police investigating this incident, taking their time and resources away from people who really needed it, but she wasn't stupid. She wouldn't return until she got the all-clear.

"Have you at least been enjoying your stay?" Sharon asked.

"I'm hardly on vacation."

"You should be. You rarely take time for yourself." Sharon rested an elbow on her desk and sat her chin in her palm. "Jocelyn said there was a car you could use while you're staying at the house?"

The owner—who apparently was Jackson Randolph's sister, of all people—did indeed have a car available. If one could refer to a Range Rover Sport as a mere "car," that is. Rachel had been nervous just sitting in its luxuriously appointed interior. The vehicle drove like a dream, though.

"Yes, there's transportation," she said grudgingly.

"Have you gotten out of the house?"

"Uh-huh."

"Wonderful. Did you go skiing at any of the resorts? Meet any hot guys?" Sharon asked, her sharp cheekbones lifting with her smile.

An image of Jackson appeared in Rachel's mind.

No. Absolutely not!

Rachel forced the vision away and flicked her eyes upward. "Concentrate on your own love life. Don't worry about mine."

"You don't have a love life—you're too busy saving the world. Even Jessica Pearson in *Suits* took a moment to indulge every once in a while, with that fine Jeff Malone."

"Jessica Pearson? Are you re-watching *Suits*?"

Sharon glanced down at something on her desk. "Isn't everyone?"

Rachel settled back against her headboard. "I date."

"Barely."

"You found your marital bliss early. For some of us, it takes a little more time."

"And a little more effort. But I'm not going to waste my

breath repeating myself. Tell me you at least did some shopping at the town square? Treated yourself to something nice?"

"Um yeah..." Rachel said. Which was true. She'd treated herself to lunch at the neighboring resort the day after she'd arrived, and she'd bought a few goodies at the Winter Market Fest. She'd also—well, Sharon didn't need to know *everything*.

Sharon tilted her head and pursed her glossed, full lips. "What did you do?"

Rachel feigned shock. "Are you accusing me of something? I'm a law-abiding citizen. I—"

"That's not what I'm talking about, and you know it. C'mon," Sharon said, pointing her finger, "what was it? Homeless shelter? Food bank? Free clinic?"

Busted.

Rachel exhaled and confessed. "A non-profit for children. Similar to the Boys & Girls Club."

"Rachel..."

"What?"

"Volunteering your time is a noble endeavor, but that's not why you're there."

"The police said I needed to get away for my safety. They didn't dictate what I should do with my time *while* I'm away."

"Of course not, but—"

"I didn't go out of my way looking for them. Someone was handing out pamphlets at the Winter Market Fest and—"

"You couldn't help yourself."

"I couldn't."

Sharon leaned forward, her expression kind. "You have a big, generous heart, but you need to listen to your head sometimes. Honestly, you can't spend your life constantly giving until you have nothing left. You need to refill your soul, too."

"Giving helps refill my soul."

"Too much of anything can be bad for you. Do me a favor?" Sharon's brown eyes gleamed through the screen. "It's the end of the year. Most people will be thinking about the giving spirit, but

I want you to be selfish. Do something frivolous, strictly for your benefit. Buy yourself something impractical, take a chance on something you've always wanted to do—skiing, maybe. Have a fling with a hot rancher. Just...try to have some fun. Please."

Rachel had never been good at being selfish or wasteful. It went against her nature and how she'd been raised. But she knew Sharon was only speaking from a place of concern. "I'll try."

"Good. I have to go. Greg and I have the Each One Teach One charity gala tonight. The Ambassador and his wife are scheduled to attend. It should be great publicity for the Foundation."

Regret that she wouldn't be there weighed as heavily as a boulder on Rachel's chest. The Each One Teach One gala was one of the few events the Turner Foundation sponsored, where local program participants could attend and meet their patrons. Rachel believed the in-person interaction was the main reason it was one of their most popular programs. Donors got to see the people who'd benefit from their contributions, which made the experience more meaningful. She looked forward to the event every year. And now she would miss it because a stalker had decided to target her.

"Have fun," she told Sharon.

"I will if you will. Enjoy the rest of your time in your very own private ski chalet."

Right. The reason she'd initially called Sharon, before the news about the police and defending her life choices had sidetracked her. "About that...it's not so private anymore."

Sharon's gaze sharpened. "What do you mean?"

"Jackson Randolph is here."

"Jackson? You mean Jocelyn's brother? Really?"

So Sharon *had* known the two were related. "That's the one. He showed up last night."

Sharon frowned. "Why on earth would he be there? He's not even supposed to be in the States. Jocelyn said he was working on some big deal in London."

"He may have been, but he's back now. And here."

"Interesting." Sharon tapped a red polished nail against her dark brown cheek. "Isn't he the guy you met at the—"

"Yes," Rachel said through clenched teeth, wishing she'd kept that particular story to herself.

"I'd totally forgotten about that when I made the arrangements with his sister." Sharon raised a perfectly groomed brow. "He's a gorgeous man."

Rachel shook her head. "No."

"You don't think he's gorgeous?"

"It's not happening."

Sharon was the epitome of wide-eyed innocence. "I'm just saying. He's good-looking, rich, and single."

"He's also an arrogant jerk. You saw the article that called out his company for being stingy with their corporate giving, right?"

"How could I not? It was everywhere."

"And do you think I'd be interested in focusing my attention on a man who doesn't share my views on philanthropy?"

"You don't have to marry him. Just have a good time."

"There isn't a good enough time in the world to make me forget all the people and causes he could've helped by being more charitable."

Sharon sighed. "I'm sorry. It's a shame his insides aren't as appealing as the package. How long will he be there?"

"I don't know. But I refuse to stay here with him. I'm looking for another place." She'd checked hotel listings, Airbnb, and VRBO this morning, but nothing in her budget was available this close to Christmas. "Despite what the police are saying, I may need to come back home."

"No way," Sharon said. "I understand staying with Jackson must be beyond awkward, but this isn't just about your comfort. It's also about your safety. Let me talk to Greg, and I'll get back to you."

"Thanks, Sharon. I appreciate the help."

Rachel ended the call and went to look out her bedroom window. Last night when she'd checked the weather app, she'd confirmed snow had been expected, but it was supposed to taper off before dawn. The app hadn't informed Mother Nature, though. Flurries fell fast and heavy, showing no signs of stopping. If anything, the dark gray sky and the thick, ominous clouds seemed to indicate more precipitation to come.

She bit her lip and glanced over her shoulder. How would that work with her reluctant roommate? Was he still asleep? Or was he awake, standing guard in the kitchen, ready to escort her from the house? He told her she'd need to leave today, but what if the weather made that impossible?

Jackson might be an asshole, but he wouldn't put her out until she had a place to go. At least, not in this weather. She'd make herself something to eat and wait to hear from Sharon. Then she could formulate a plan for when the snow stopped.

If it stopped.

With one last worried look out the window, she grabbed her phone and left the safety of her bedroom.

Chapter Three

Three days until Christmas...

Jackson rubbed his brow and stared in disbelief at the thick snowflakes plummeting from the sky, creating a panoramic landscape of white that stretched as far as the eye could see. He turned to address Rachel, who sat at the kitchen's marble-topped island counter across the room, her back to him.

"Did you know this storm was coming?"

Rachel lifted the coffee cup in her hand and took a sip before responding. "No. It surprised me, too."

He shoved both hands through his hair, frustration roiling within him. He shouldn't have taken those pills. Between the pain meds, his fatigue from travel, and his jet lag, he'd slept over thirty-six hours. Not continuously, though. He groggily recalled gaining consciousness several times to stumble to the bathroom or to drink the fresh glass of water he'd found waiting on the nightstand. Still, when he'd finally roused, he'd been starving and unable to believe he'd lost a full day.

Or that the weather had devolved to such a degree.

"It looks like a fucking blizzard out there."

"Probably because that's what it is," Rachel said, dryly. "The news has taken to calling it Snowmageddon."

"This can't happen today." Maybe if he said it enough times, the blizzard would magically resolve itself.

"Why? Because it makes it harder for you to kick me out?"

He winced. Right. He'd planned to address their current living situation as soon as he saw her this morning, but the weather, and the problems it would cause, had blasted everything else from his mind.

He turned away from the growing whiteout and jammed his hands into his pockets. "I'm sorry. I shouldn't have said that last night, especially when I didn't mean it. I wouldn't have made you leave."

"It was the night before," she said primly before murmuring, "And so you say *now*."

She swung around on the stool until she faced him. Her leggings were a colorful patterned fabric that stretched over her shapely legs, and a slouchy sweatshirt bared one smooth shoulder. She'd pulled her curls up until they sat like a crown on top of her head.

He swallowed. Rachel looked sexier in lounging clothes than most women looked in lingerie.

Focus, Jackson.

"Did the meteorologists say how long they expected it to snow?" he asked, forcing a casual tone into his voice.

"On and off until Christmas Eve."

"Two more days?" Christ! If he hustled, the trip was still doable.

"Until the storm moves out of the area."

"I doubt the Land Rover will get through snow this deep. I guess I could call the car service I used to bring me from the airport. And if they plow the road soon, I could make my flight tonight."

"Uh... I'm not sure the county's plows will get to us by then."

The sensation of cold fingers grazed the back of his neck at her words. "What does that mean?" He lived in DC. They got snow, although nothing like this, and when they did, people were usually out and about the following day.

Rachel's brow furrowed. "We're the only house on this mountain. We're not a top priority."

Not a top priority? Since when? He cocked a brow. "I'll call someone in county administration."

She wrinkled her nose. "That's not the way it works. Interstates and roads that have the highest volume of traffic are cleared first, followed by those that are most traveled. The county will then give precedence to roads that lead to hospitals, and then the resorts and the shopping districts, because those places could suffer an economic disadvantage if they aren't cleared."

He would suffer an economic disadvantage if he couldn't get out of here. And not just him. All his employees, and their families, and... He sighed. "If the county can't get to us, I'll pay a private company."

Rachel scoffed. "You can't throw money at everything."

"Why not? It works."

"Typical." She pursed her lips. "This is a large area. The county's resources will be taxed. They could decide to close all nonessential roads until they have the available manpower and equipment. What would your private company do then? Their snow removal truck wouldn't even get up here until the county opens the road."

He scraped a hand through his hair. "And how do you know all of this?"

"You'd be surprised by what you learn when you volunteer for women shelters that rely on daily deliveries for food. Besides, with blizzard conditions, it isn't safe to drive, anyway. And I seriously doubt any planes will be cleared to fly." She sighed and slid off the stool. "I'm going to see what supplies we have."

Jackson gritted his teeth and closed his eyes. This couldn't be happening. Maybe he'd just thought he'd awakened but he was actually in some pill-popping induced nightmare. Any second now, he'd wake up to chilly but sunny conditions.

Three... two...

He opened his eyes.

Still snowing.

This was not good. He was supposed to leave for Portland today, a trip that was integral to the future success of his company. While RRG was still extremely profitable, Jackson knew that trends regarding retail and brick and mortar stores were changing. People were just as likely to order goods online, bolstered by reviews or social media recommendations, as they were to leave the comfort of their homes and go to a mall. Not wanting to be on the tail end of a major shift in the market, he'd started working on the integration of technology and retail, mainly ways it could streamline the in-store experience. His team had come up with a prototype and had chosen Portland to be the test market. It had taken months, but they'd managed to get the support of the Portland city council.

The shopping center would be the crown jewel in RRG's new plan to target Gen Z and the newer generation of consumers. Being the first to market was essential to his plan to brand RRG as the developer of this new breed of shopping centers. If it worked, RRG would be set for decades to come. He'd have done his part to protect the Randolph legacy.

The way his grandfather always wanted.

However, when the corporate giving story hit, the council began to balk at their prior approval. If his company lost this opportunity, it'd be back to the drawing board with another city, a move that could set them back years. He had one shot to get to Portland's mayor and city manager before the holiday began. One shot to allay their concerns about RRG and assure them the story was just a holiday distraction that would soon disappear. If he waited until the new year, without a counter to the article's allegations, there was a good chance they'd pull their support. He couldn't allow that to happen.

But how was he going to stop it in the face of this weather?

Jackson walked over to the kitchen counter and braced his

hands on the gleaming marble. This entire situation was unbelievable. Why hadn't he gone back to DC after London, instead of allowing Joss to convince him to hide away here? If he had, he wouldn't be in this mess. The weather mess, not the company's damaged reputation mess.

He wasn't ashamed of the decisions he'd made for RRG. It wasn't a charity. It was a business. A designation that could've been challenged considering the condition of the company when he'd taken over seven years ago. He wouldn't let it fall back into that state. Where they'd been content merely to exist, not thrive.

He couldn't be stranded here—his attendance at the meeting was imperative. He'd hire a helicopter to set down in the back yard if he had to.

"It's not that bad. We're lucky it isn't worse," Rachel said, coming back into the great room, a piece of paper in her hand.

"I don't see how that's possible. We could be stuck here for five or six days."

"We've known that for an hour." She snapped her fingers in front of his face. "Get with it, Jack. The time for whining has passed."

He grabbed her wrist, and her eyes flew to his. He was instantly aware of her enticing scent, and his fingers tingled where they rested against her skin. A flush colored her cheeks and worked its way down to her collarbone.

Ah, there it was. That look.

When he'd first emerged from his bedroom, her gaze had darted over him, taking him in from head to toe before she'd narrowed her eyes and turned away. But he'd seen it.

That look. The one that said she liked what she was seeing and wouldn't mind seeing more.

The look that had left little brush fires in its wake.

"I don't whine," he murmured, sweeping his thumb against her throbbing pulse.

She was right, though. When faced with their current predicament, he'd wasted time complaining before looking for ways to plot his escape. Meanwhile, she'd focused on determining if they'd have the supplies needed to survive while they were here.

She was unlike any woman he'd ever known. The women he'd dated in the past would've been freaking out or flopping around, unaware of the possible dangers of their situation. Of course, to be fair to them, he hadn't dated them for their intellect. He'd wanted his relationships to be easy and uncomplicated. That would allow him to put all his focus on RRG.

Rachel was anything but easy and uncomplicated. It was why being with her had invigorated him.

But acknowledging her virtues wasn't helpful to his cause in this situation. It only served to make him horny as hell.

She tugged her arm, and he immediately released her. She cleared her throat and licked her lips. "I was talking about the supplies, not the weather."

"What did you find?" His voice emerged husky.

Rachel lowered her lashes and read from her list. "We have milk, eggs, bread, meats, frozen pizzas, frozen hors d'oeuvres, pasta and sauce, mac n' cheese, and canned soup. Enough to last us at least two weeks. I think we could stretch it if we needed to be here longer."

"Two weeks? I can't be stuck here with you that long!"

She flinched and her eyes widened, the hurt in them unmistakable until she quickly masked it.

What was wrong with him? He was constantly sticking his size eleven-and-a-halves in his mouth when it came to Rachel. Which was the last thing he wanted to do when there were other parts he yearned to put in *her*.

He squeezed his eyes shut and pinched the bridge of his nose. "I'm sorry. I didn't mean it like that."

"You're such a sweet talker," she said, her tone dripping with acid.

"Trust me, this isn't about you. I need to be in Portland no later than Christmas Eve, and now it looks like I won't make it."

"What's in Portland?"

He averted his gaze, not willing to get into the details. "A very important business meeting."

"Oh yeah, sounds like life or death." She sighed. "I'm hoping they'll get to us by the day *after* Christmas."

Two could play the insult game. "Why? So you can go shopping?"

"No. A local charity sponsors an after-the-holidays toy drive. I agreed to help."

Her snide, condescending attitude grated. "You just got here, and you've already adopted a local charity? Doesn't it get tiresome carrying Mother Teresa's mantle?"

"At least I'm trying to help people instead of losing my shit over a business meeting."

"A very important business meeting," he reiterated. "And me making that meeting benefits others, like my employees and my stockholders."

She crossed her arms over her chest. "I hardly think they count as less fortunate."

"Why? Because only people who are poor, homeless, and marginalized deserve your compassion?"

"Yes!"

He was so sick of this attitude from people who assumed big business and wealth were the antithesis of all things good in the world.

"Do you know who else I'm responsible for?" he ground out. "Who else I'm referring to when I talk about our stockholders? It's not just the rich elites. It's my employees; people who've worked for RRG for years. Who have company stock in their 401Ks and pensions. Seven years ago, the pension fund had lost more than half its value. Now, it's higher than ever. Those people will be able to retire with something in the bank because of what I've done at RRG. The decisions I make affect thousands of people."

A blush dotted her cheekbones. "I didn't think about that. I'm sorry."

He nodded. "Thank you."

She waited, an aura of expectation hovering over her, like she was waiting for *him* to express his regret. She'd be waiting for a while. He'd already apologized for what he'd done wrong.

Her lips tightened, but she didn't pursue it. Instead, she sighed and said, "The house runs on gas heat and there's a back-up generator, so we shouldn't lose power. Add the food to that and we have everything we need until the county plows the road."

How could she be so calm about this? So accepting? Everything had spiraled out of his control ever since that damn article came out. People, companies, the media...he'd been responding to each new disaster, always on defense. And now she wanted him to sit and wait for someone to come get him?

No more.

He was tired of reacting to things. It was time for him to act.

Determination fueled his muscles. He strode past Rachel, with her arched brows and gaping mouth, through the kitchen to the mudroom on the side of the house. One wall held neatly stacked skis and snowboards, while built-in cubbies stuffed with assorted snow gear lined two others.

He grabbed a familiar-looking pair of boots and a thick pair of socks, then sat down on the bench in the middle of the room.

"What do you think you're doing?" Rachel asked, standing in the doorway, her fists jammed on her hips.

That's right. He was *doing* something. And damn if it didn't feel good.

He tugged on the socks, then reached for the black insulated pants with high back suspenders. "I'm going to walk out and survey our situation. Maybe I can tell if our road has been closed, or if they've started treating it."

"You're being ridiculous. We're in the middle of a storm."

He jerked his head to indicate the small rectangular windows above the cubbies. "Didn't you notice? The snow has stopped."

"For *now!* But they're expecting more. You don't know when

it'll start again, and with this wind, you won't be able to see how to get back if it does."

She didn't understand. If he wasn't going to make it to Portland in time, possibly jeopardizing his plans for his company, then he needed to make sure he'd exhausted every possible option to leave. That he'd overlooked nothing.

With the massive ball of guilt and frustration crushing his chest, he stepped into the boots and explained himself as best as he could in that moment. "I can't just *sit* here."

Her expression softened. Maybe he'd finally gotten through to her. "And what happens if you go out there and get lost or hurt?" she asked. "Did you forget about your leg?"

No. The dull ache had been present all morning, but a full day and a half of sleep had done wonders. That and the handful of ibuprofen he'd swallowed before coming into the kitchen. He wasn't about to take another of the major pain pills.

He straightened and removed the matching black jacket from its hook. "I'll be fine. And I won't go far."

"What in the world was I thinking?" she muttered, looking skyward. Then, "You're being idiotic, but have at it," she said, flinging a hand toward the door before stalking away from him.

He stared after her, wishing the situation were different. He wished he could follow her, scoop her up in his arms, and finish what they'd started all those months ago. That they could spend the day in bed or in front of the fireplace, their only concern being whose turn it was to refill their drinks or get more food. That they could have more of those stimulating debates that had sent them scrambling into the cloakroom, unable to keep their hands off each other one moment longer.

He scrubbed a hand over his face. But that wasn't how their story would play out. And after everything he'd said and done, he was pretty sure all he'd ever have of Rachel Williams were memories. He'd made his decision. He had to see it through.

He zipped up his jacket, grabbed a hat, gloves, and a visor, and stomped over to the door. When he pulled it open, a gust of wind added to his force, almost knocking him down. A sizable amount of snow deposited itself on the tile floor. He took a deep breath and headed out, closing the door behind him.

Dark gray clouds blanketed the sky but as he'd seen, it was no longer snowing. The wind whistled in his ear, blocking out any other sound and causing swirls of fluffy powder to drift around him. It was white for as far as he could see.

Beautiful.

He imagined it would've been soothing to take in from inside, in front of a roaring fire with a hot toddy in one hand and Rachel curled on his lap.

Too late now, Randolph. Get moving.

He took off, trudging around to the front of the property. The house had been constructed in a manner that blocked a lot of snow from piling on the side door. Unfortunately, the main walkway hadn't been afforded that same protection. At least a foot of the powdery stuff covered the walkway.

More like eighteen inches, he amended, when he stepped into it and sank down to just above his calf. He attempted to plow through it, but several feet in, he'd resorted to a modified hop scramble, leading with his good leg, which his bad knee did not like at all.

Pain is temporary. Portland is the start of forever.

He repeated his own personal mantra as he continued following the walkway. He was usually in great shape, devoting five days a week to a grueling workout in a downtown gym near his office, but the last couple of weeks had taken their toll, and each high step required a ton of strength and energy he no longer had. And because he'd been concentrating so hard on his forward momentum, he'd failed to notice the snow whipping around his head wasn't due to the wind, but because it had started falling again.

He stopped and took a deep breath, raising a hand to shield his eyes. It was coming down steadily and he hadn't even made it to the main gate, usually a few minutes by car. He'd been out here long enough that he should've reached it by now.

Hadn't he?

Maybe he'd underestimated how long he'd been walking. With the conditions deteriorating and his difficulty moving, it was entirely possible that what felt to him like half an hour had only been several minutes. That seemed to be borne out by the fact that he could no longer feel the ache in his knee. Which was probably a good thing. Because he *was* icing it.

Technically.

Should he keep going? The main gate couldn't be much farther. Or should he return to the house and try again when the snow stopped?

He turned, expecting to see the lights from the house, but all he saw was a blanket of wildly falling snow.

Where was the house?

Panic gripped his chest and squeezed, but Jackson fought not to give in to it. If he retraced his steps, he'd find his way back.

Only—

The snow was whipping and swirling around him so vigorously that he could barely see his feet, much less his trail. He bent to get a better look and realized the impressions he'd made were quickly being filled in.

He tipped his head back and gazed upward toward the nonexistent sky. He hated to admit it, but Rachel was right—he shouldn't have left the house. But he couldn't dwell on that now, and more importantly, he couldn't remain out here. If he did, he'd freeze to death. His best chance was to turn around and pray his sense of direction would lead him back to the chalet.

Many minutes later, when he still couldn't see the lights of the house, he knew he was well and truly fucked.

Indecision plagued him, a state of being that was unfamiliar.

Should he keep going and risk heading farther and farther from the house? Or should he stay where he was and wait for things to clear up so he could find his way?

Was this divine justice? The media would spin it as such: *Weeks after his company made the corporate Grinch list, Jackson Randolph IV died in a snowstorm. And that, ladies and gentlemen, is what we call karma.*

Was that how he'd be remembered? The sudden realization that he'd only be missed by his sister and his employees' pension plans struck him as depressing. Is that what he'd sacrificed everything for? Would the sum of his life's worth come down to some malls and town centers? Was that the legacy he wanted to leave behind?

He pictured Rachel back at the house. Smart, beautiful, passionate, giving Rachel. Had she begun to worry about him? Or had she not spared him a second thought? He couldn't blame her. He'd been a complete and utter ass to her. Which was ridiculous when all he'd wanted to do was pull her close and kiss her, the way he'd done in that cloakroom all those months ago.

If he managed to make it out of this alive, he'd tell her how he felt. He'd admit how much their differences intrigued him, how her conviction forced him to consider other perspectives, and how hurt he'd been by her rejection.

And he'd do whatever it took to convince her to give him another chance.

The wind howled, and Jackson pulled his hat down over his ears. He managed a few more steps. Stopped. This was it. He didn't know where he was going. Proceeding would be suicide. Staying still, he'd freeze to death.

He thought about Rachel. The warmth of her heated gaze, her skin glowing in the flickering firelight, and that husky laugh. He'd never see her again.

He'd taken a risk by leaving the chalet.

He'd lost.

Chapter Four

Rachel was so mad she could scream. Who went off walking in the middle of a blizzard? Obviously, someone selfish who only cared about his own needs. So why should she have expected anything different from Jackson? If he were a thoughtful, considerate person, his company wouldn't have been called out for being uncharitable. Not to mention her own personal experience with him when he'd left her high and dry—ok, wet, but she stood by the expression!—in that cloakroom six months ago.

She stood before the large windows, her arms crossed over her chest, staring out at the expanse of white in the distance.

The kettle finally whistled. She straightened, turned the burner off, and grabbed an oversized ceramic mug and a box of herbal tea out of the cabinet.

It would've served him right if she hadn't gone after him. She'd explained the dangers of the storm and the unlikelihood of anyone getting to them anytime soon. And still, he'd chosen to leave. She pursed her lips. If he'd wanted to ignore what she'd said and waste his time traipsing around in the snow, then, like that old school Bobby Brown song, that was his prerogative.

She sank onto the sofa, grabbed a popular food magazine

from the coffee table, and flipped through the pages until she got tired of feigning interest in the recipes and tossed it back on the stack. She grabbed the remote and powered on the TV, only to turn it off at the nonstop coverage of Snowmageddon. It had taken over twenty minutes but the break in the storm had finally passed, and the snow was falling heavier and heavier.

She tried to swallow past the worry tightening her throat. She could barely see beyond the window. Where was Jackson? Had he returned? Or was he—

Not allowing herself to complete the thought, she raced into the well-stocked mudroom that could've been mistaken for the showroom of a high-end camping emporium. It was empty. No signs of discarded clothing or boots; only a pile of snow melting into a large puddle of water.

Chills that had nothing to do with the weather rippled through her body.

He wasn't here. He hadn't made it back. Which meant he was still out there and might need her help.

She suppressed the panic that threatened to send her to a corner curling into the fetal position. She needed to calm down and formulate a plan. Though time was precious, it would do neither of them any good if she blindly rushed out and they both ended up in trouble. Taking stock of the available supplies, she quickly donned the most colorful snowsuit she could find and matching boots. She grabbed half a dozen ski poles, several coils of rope, a heavy-duty flashlight, and ventured out into her own personal frozen tundra.

Hold on, Jackson. I'm coming.

The cloud cover was thick, rendering the entire landscape gray, but it was only mid-afternoon, meaning her surroundings were light. She slowly moved along the side of the house, the wind pushing against her like it had a personal vendetta. When she reached the front porch, she tied the end of a rope around a wooden spindle on the railing. She marched several yards from the house, jammed another ski pole in the snow, looped the rope through its handle, and forged ahead, repeating the process.

If it were night, she doubted she would see him. She shuddered to think about what might have occurred. But there, ahead, she could just barely make out his black-clad hooded figure which stood motionless, as if frozen in place. The strength of the emotions that tumbled forth almost overwhelmed her.

Relief. Frustration. A tinge of anger. And desire... mixed with an extreme level of gratitude that the man she'd met six months ago—the man who'd charmed her off that bar stool and into the cloakroom with his intellect and sense of humor—was okay.

The intensity of her feelings gave her the fortitude to erase the last bit of distance between them. He hadn't veered too far off the path, but she could see how he'd gotten disoriented. How fifty yards from the house could seem like fifty miles.

But it wouldn't have happened if he'd stayed put.

It was a testament to the ferociousness of the storm that he didn't seem to notice her until she was several feet away. He straightened and jerked forward when she reached for him.

"Come with me if you want to live." Hearing the words, she huffed out a laugh. "I can't believe I said that."

An hour later, Rachel dropped an herbal tea bag into an oversized ceramic mug, filled it with hot water from the kettle, and took it into the great room. Jack sat on the sofa, wrapped in a camel and beige sherpa fleece blanket, staring into the crackling fire.

He'd discarded the snowsuit and boots in the mudroom and changed into a pair of long-sleeved navy cotton pajamas she'd found folded in her closet.

"Thank you," he said in a ragged voice, accepting the hot beverage.

It was the first words he'd spoken since they'd gotten back to the house. His face was ashen, and his hands trembled slightly as he raised the drink to his lips. He looked vulnerable and unguarded in a way she'd never have imagined if she weren't seeing it with her own eyes.

And sexy. Despite everything he'd gone through, he still looked devastatingly attractive. Damn him.

She shook her head. "You'll be lucky if your ass doesn't end up with hypothermia."

He cautiously swallowed a sip and looked up at her, his blue eyes somber. "I know."

But there was no putting the cork back in the bottle. The words tumbled forth, spurred on by irritation and adrenaline. "Of all the stupid, asinine things to do. You could've killed us both."

"I know."

"Did you really think I would stay in the house and not come after you? Do you think I could've lived with myself if something had happened to you, and I hadn't made—"

"Rachel!" His voice was forceful enough to cut through her rant, but not harsh. "You're right. It was stupid, insane, foolish, and any other word you want to throw at me. I *know*, and I'm sorry."

His admission deflated her anger. "I get it; you have someplace else you'd rather be. But you're stuck here—and we're stuck with each other—until the storm is over and the roads are cleared."

"I don't object to being here with you. I was focused on—" He broke off as a visible shiver wracked his frame. "Damn, I can't seem to stay warm."

Shame soured the back of her throat.

Nice going, Rachel. Any sick kids you want to yell at? Puppies you want to kick?

The fire in the fireplace roared and popped, sending additional heat out into the room. But it wasn't enough.

She gently took the mug from him before he could spill its contents and placed it on the side table. She sat down next to him on the sofa. "Scoot over."

He did, pulling on the blanket so it fanned out to encompass her. "I knew you couldn't resist me," he said, his teeth beginning to chatter.

That was the Jack she knew and—

She sighed. "Just shut up, would you?" She tucked herself against his side and put her arms around him as best she could, considering how broad he was. This close, she could see how sweat had curled his hair against the nape of his neck and the stubble covering his cheeks was on the verge of sprouting into a beard.

She placed her chin on his shoulder. Her outrage was ebbing, laying bare the true emotion gripping her insides and twisting her chest.

Fear.

"I've never been that scared before in my life," she whispered. Including the recent incident that was the cause for her own presence in the chalet.

Regret surged through her. He could've died and it would have been because she'd practically egged him out of the door. She never would've approached anyone else that way. She would've tried to help them find another course of action to meet their goal. But not with Jack.

Why?

Because her feelings had been hurt.

Or was it because she resented the feelings that he aroused in her?

"Have you always been this stubborn?" she asked.

"That's what I've been told," he said, his eyes closed, his lashes resting on his skin.

"Your stubbornness mixed with my inflexibility. Unstoppable force, immovable object," she muttered.

"That's one of the many things I admire about you," he said in a low voice.

He shivered and turned toward her, sliding one arm behind her lower back and snuggling down until his head rested above her breasts. Her nipples immediately tightened, and her heart thumped in her chest. She grimaced at her body's inappropriate response.

This is not the time, Rachel!

As the minutes passed, his tremors lessened and his breathing grew deeper, his chest rising and falling steadily. She slid her fingers through the short strands of his hair and allowed herself a moment to study him freely.

God, he was beautiful, in that way that seemed unapproachable or too good to be true. Maybe it was the perfect symmetry of his features…or the way the firelight lovingly traced the angles of his cheekbones, the strong slash of his jaw, the straight line of his nose. Whatever the reason, she was tempted to remain here for the foreseeable future, the heat from his bulk warming her in a way that had nothing to do with being cold.

And that was the impetus for her slipping out of his embrace and from beneath the blanket. She would check the rest of the house, make some calls, and start preparing dinner.

She'd risen and taken a step when his hand shot out and tugged her back down onto his lap.

She froze. "Jack?"

"Jackson." His voice rumbled against her back. "My name is Jackson, but you keep calling me Jack."

Because she knew he hated it and irritating him was a good way to create distance, which she desperately needed. The heat from his chest seared through her shirt and his thighs were solid beneath her. The unexpected nearness short-circuited her brain.

She sucked in a deep breath and ordered her gray matter to keep up. "And you're not asleep. Now that we're both done stating basic facts, you want to let me up?"

"Not really. I like having you near me. You're warm and cozy."

She liked being near him. Too much. Which is why she'd heeded the self-preserving warning to move away. Still, the man had almost frozen to death. Sure, it was his own doing, but she couldn't deny him warmth because his proximity sent her mind and body in a direction that neither could afford to go. "Okay, but just for a little while."

She hadn't been this close to him since the night of the fundraiser. When lingering glances, low voices and fleeting touches had led to long, slow, drugging kisses, heavy breathing, and intimate caresses in a small, dark room.

Even now, the memory affected her body, causing her skin to flush, her nerves to tingle, and an aching warmth to settle low in her belly.

C'mon, think! Talk about something—anything—else.

"What was so important that you would risk getting yourself killed?" she blurted out.

His muscles went rigid beneath her.

"Sorry." It was clear that she could sit there or she could talk; it was too much to ask for her to do both. Because she wanted an answer to her question, she slid off his lap to a safer position a full cushion away from him, tucking her feet beneath her. "What I'm trying to say is I want to understand why you were willing to do what you did. Why going to Portland is so crucial."

He sighed, as if missing her heat, then straightened and opened his eyes. "My grandfather, Jackson Randolph, Jr., started Rand Realty Group in 1949. For almost six decades, he worked to build RRG into a trusted national brand. The fact that our name was synonymous with quality development was something he was extremely proud of."

Rachel couldn't help but be moved by the affection and respect in Jackson's voice as he talked about his grandfather.

"After Grandpop died, my father took over. He was a good man and a good father, but business wasn't his forte. Truth be told, he had no interest in running the company. And it showed. The company lost more than three-quarters of its value during the eight years he was at the helm. By the time I took over seven years ago, we were floundering. Badly. It took hard work and sacrifice, but I managed to restore RRG's prominence in the industry."

"That's wonderful, but I don't see what that has to do with—"

"We can't rest on our laurels," he said, shifting on his hip to face her. "That's how my father chose to run the company, and it's how we got into trouble. If we want to remain relevant, we need to adapt to the times. My meetings in Portland were going to help with that, but then this irresponsible article came out, smearing my company and my grandfather's name. Portland started to balk, and I—"

"Lost your damn mind?" she volunteered.

"Yeah, I guess I did." He hesitated, then said, "You know that article was bogus, right?"

How would she know that? Other than a couple of hours spent with him months before, she didn't know anything about him. Besides, the article seemed well researched. She arched a brow. "Really? So RRG gave more than point seven percent of their revenue last year?"

Jack rubbed the back of his neck. "Who made *Living thru Giving* the arbiter over what is appropriate philanthropic behavior for corporations to make?"

Somebody needed to hold these corporations accountable, and she applauded the site for their efforts, even though it was damaging Jack in the process. Maybe it'd force him to do better next year.

"Twenty million dollars is a lot of money to a lot of people, but when you make close to three billion, it's a drop in a bucket," she said. "An insult. To you, it's another blinged-out watch, a yacht, or some insanely expensive car, but to a worthy recipient it can mean life or death."

His lips twisted, and he slowly shook his head. "I told you about my grandfather and how hard I worked to honor his memory and you think I'd rather spend money on a watch than give to people in need?"

She bit her lip and looked away from his censorious gaze. Had she gone too far in her assumptions? "But the article said—"

"Yes, that's the amount we gave in straight cash donations to charity," he admitted, his irritation obvious. "But that doesn't encompass all we do. The fact that I don't hold a press conference or make a photo op out of it doesn't mean we're not contributing."

Fight flared up in her again. "I don't care about photo ops, either. But I do care that we live in a society that deifies the acquisition of wealth, no matter who's harmed in the process."

"Making money isn't a bad thing. I'm not going to apologize for doing my job."

"No one's asking you to apologize, just to be mindful of ways you can help those who are less fortunate than you."

"This is what drives me crazy about this whole situation," he said, blowing out a sharp breath. "People are willing to vilify RRG and me without considering all the facts. Quick sound bites have replaced comprehensive news stories." He scrubbed both hands over his face. "Could we do more? Absolutely. And I'll be the first to admit that I've had tunnel vision for the past seven years. All I could think about was rebuilding my grandfather's company and restoring honor back to his name."

"And you did that," she said softly.

"At a cost I didn't anticipate, apparently. It's not that I don't believe in giving back. We do give in ways that's more than writing a check. We've donated computers and other tech equipment to the city's public libraries and elementary and middle schools. We grant competitive scholarships to children of RRG employees. We provide resources and funds to local non-profit grassroots organizations working to reduce homelessness in the District. And we have a program where we offer quality temporary housing to families displaced by the city when their living conditions are deemed unsafe. Unlike others, we don't issue a press release each time we do it."

Rachel blinked. Maybe they should, because that sounded amazing. She worked in DC's philanthropic sector and she hadn't heard about his company carrying out any of those efforts. He might have a point about the article. "I didn't realize—"

"But most importantly," he said with emphasis, "we pay well, offer great benefits, and support our employee's professional development. Additionally, our offices have significantly reduced our carbon footprint, are mostly paper-free, and offer flexible work from home options when applicable. Shouldn't that count for something? Would people be happier if we publicly donated millions more and yet we treated our workers poorly? Or harmed the environment with our development practices?"

"No. But it's possible to do both." She leaned toward him, jazzed about a topic she'd been currently researching in her own work. "You mentioned keeping up with the times. Have you ever considered the business you may be losing by *not* advertising your giving? Especially with millennials and Gen Z?"

He frowned. "No."

"Young people today care more about giving back than the prior two generations. They prefer to work for and give their money to businesses that contribute to causes that interest them. I'm not suggesting you should donate to Portland's number one charity and hold a press conference about it; they'll see right through that. But if you identify a few institutions that tie directly into your area of expertise, establish an authentic relationship, and set up a consistent practice of giving, you'll reap the rewards. Professionally and personally. And the more you give, the more you'll come to love the feeling you get from giving."

Admiration brightened his features, and he leaned in. "That's a great idea. You've given me a lot to think about. And speaking of thinking..." He rested his cheek against the back of the sofa and lowered his voice. "I've thought about our time together often in the past few months. You don't know how much I regretted leaving you the way I did."

She'd thought about it, too. Marveled over how she'd been that attracted to someone she'd just met. She still found it incredible that she'd let her guard down, or that she'd been as crushed as she was when she'd discovered his identity.

He reached out and trailed his fingers along the back of her hand. "I hurried back as quick as I could, but when I did, you were gone."

Rachel sucked in a quick breath. "When we first met, I didn't know who you were."

One corner of his mouth tilted upward. "As I recall, we didn't talk much about ourselves."

That had been part of the allure and had added to the erotic quality of the experience. They'd been two strangers who'd met, connected, and allowed themselves to indulge in the sexiness of that anonymity.

But then she'd found out who he was, the knowledge bursting into the dome of sensuality that had encased them, leaving her keenly aware, and regretful, of what she'd almost done.

"After you left, I heard someone greet you and mention your company and a recent project. I realized you were one of the businessmen at the fundraiser that I'd been sent to pitch to. And that you were probably like them; more interested in lining your own pockets than helping others in need. It spooked me. I figured we had nothing in common. It seemed easier to stop things before they started."

His eyes widened. "*That's* why you never returned my calls or texts? I thought it was because I'd left."

"I often wondered how you got my phone number. I don't remember giving it to you."

"Once I had your name, getting your number wasn't difficult." He yawned, then winced.

And just like, that she knew their discussion was done. She rose. "Are you hungry?"

"Not really."

"Me, neither. But I'll make something in case either of us changes our mind later. Are you going to be alright?"

He exhaled heavily. "Yeah, I should be fine. I think I'm going to sit here for a while, and then I'm going to take a long, warm shower."

Great! Now images of him standing naked beneath the spray as suds ran down his broad chest, flat stomach, and even lower would be running on a loop in her mind for the rest of the night. She cleared her throat. "Uh... okay."

She headed to the kitchen.

"Rachel?"

She stopped and turned to find he'd stood and wrapped the blanket around him so that only his face was visible. "Yeah?"

His heated stare burned across the room. "You were right. I shouldn't have gone out there. So why did you come after me?"

It was funny: Sharon had asked her the same thing after her run-in with the man outside her apartment. *"You knew it was a dangerous situation. You could've been seriously hurt. Why did you do it?"*

She shrugged. "You needed me, and I was in a position to help. It's what I do."

Jack shook his head. "But you could've been injured."

"What would it say about me if I'd sat in the house and *you'd* ended up injured, lost, or worse?"

"It would say that of the two of us, you were exercising the common sense I was lacking."

Ha! If that were true, she'd be doing her best to keep her distance instead of lamenting the fact that they weren't different people, and he currently wasn't in the condition to pick up where they'd left off six months ago.

Chapter Five

Two days until Christmas...

The following morning, a ray of sun fell across Jackson's face, awakening him. He lay in the bed, allowing himself a moment to take stock of his body. His lower back ached and there was still a slight twinge in his knee, but physically, he was feeling much better than he had in a few days.

He lifted his forearm across his eyes, blocking the glare. He didn't deserve to feel this good, considering what he'd done. What in the hell had he been thinking, traipsing out in the middle of a snowstorm? He couldn't believe he'd actually convinced himself he could help by checking on conditions. His actions had almost "helped" him and Rachel into early graves.

But coming close to dying in a blizzard had also provided him the opportunity for some much-needed clarity. He hadn't forgotten what he'd promised himself out there in the snow: to tell Rachel how he felt and ask her for a second chance. He'd made some progress after the rescue yesterday. During a time of vulnerability, he'd let down his guard and had received a chance to be close to Rachel again. He'd confessed his hopes, his fears, and his frustrations, and he thought it had brought them closer.

He planned to further nurture that closeness today.

He stood, stretched, and padded over to the bedroom window that faced the chalet's side yard. Thin, wispy clouds stretched across the bright blue sky and sunshine reflected off the smooth white canvas of snow. It looked harmless and peaceful now, like something out of the Earth documentary or a screen saver image. But Jackson had learned the dangers were all too real and that he'd never take them for granted again.

He went into the adjourning bathroom, splashed some water on his face, and brushed his teeth. Then he pulled on a shirt and a pair of joggers.

He picked up his phone. "Siri! Call Joss."

A moment later, his sister answered. "Hey! Are you on your way to Portland?"

"Nope. Slight change in plans."

"What happened?"

"Snowmageddon."

"Oh no," Joss said. "What are you going to do about the meeting?"

Jackson frowned. His sister's words tracked, but there was something about her tone that seemed, well...off. "There's nothing I can do about it now," he said slowly.

"That's too bad."

He was probably imagining things. Another reason he wasn't keen to spend the next few days stressing about Portland. It wasn't a healthy mindset for him, as his behavior the day before had shown. Besides, there was something else that required his undivided focus.

"Do you know someone named Rachel Williams?"

"Who? You'd need to be more specific." His sister's voice faded out and strengthened again. "That's not a unique name."

"She works at the Turner Foundation."

"Oh, yeah. Sharon Gilmore's assistant. We've met." Her words were low and unintelligible before she continued. "I believe they were invited to our fundraiser back in June."

He looked at the full bars, showing a strong signal. He'd been right. Something was up. "Jocelyn Randolph Hutchinson, what is going on?" he demanded.

"What are you talking about?" Joss asked, though her words lacked the usual conviction.

"What are you not telling me?"

"Okay, okay," she said, giving in way too easily. She mumbled something he couldn't understand, then— "I know...Yes, I will." She cleared her throat. "Brad wanted me to tell you that you have the right to be annoyed, but do watch what you say to his wife."

So whatever Joss was hiding, his brother-in-law was in on it, too?

"I knew that you'd asked around about her," Joss said. "That you got her phone number."

He didn't bother to ask how she found out. She always had, even when they were growing up. She'd claimed it was her older sister special powers.

"Why didn't you say anything?"

"Because I didn't want to jinx it. It was the first time in years where you were interested in something outside of RRG."

His usual defensiveness kicked in. "The company was in bad shape when I took over."

"I know, but you've ate, slept, and breathed RRG for the past seven years. That company won't keep you warm at night."

Not the way Rachel had yesterday.

"I went looking for you when you slipped out of the fundraiser back in June," Joss continued. "I saw the two of you talking at the bar. The chemistry was evident and unmistakable, even from where I was standing. After that night, you asked around, got her phone number, and then...nothing. Crickets."

He should've known this type of coincidence was too great to occur naturally.

"Did you know she was here when you suggested I lie low at your place instead of back in DC?"

"Maybe," she said, her inflection rising with the last syllable.

That would be a "yes." He had another, less palatable thought. "Did you have anything to do with that charity article?"

"No!" she cried, her response swift and forceful. "I would never have done that. That article was pure bullshit."

"Most of it," he agreed. But Rachel had made some solid points yesterday, and he planned to give them serious thought when he returned home.

If he'd known before he'd arrived here that Joss had arranged this set-up, he would've been furious. Hence his brother-in-law's warning. But now—

"Thanks, Joss."

There was a small pause and then she said, "You're welcome. So, it's going well?"

"It was a little rough in the beginning, but I have high hopes."

"Good. Now, you guys should be okay there for a while. In addition to the shopping Amelia did before she left, there's a box of more dry goods in the storage room and...a surprise."

Jackson was stunned at what his sister had pulled off. "What if I hadn't called?"

"We were counting on one of you to reach out to us before the holidays."

We?

Joss answered his unspoken question by adding, "I'll call Sharon and let her know it's all working out so far. Merry Christmas, little brother."

"Not yet, but it might be. I'll call you soon."

While he was grateful for his sister's efforts, he knew the rest was up to him.

Leaving his room, he glanced to the right. Rachel's door was still closed. He stared at it for a long time before he went left and headed into the great room. Had he even thanked her for what she'd done? If not, he planned to rectify that oversight as soon as possible.

He grabbed two coffee mugs and a couple of pods and began

making coffee. As it brewed, he looked in the refrigerator to see what he could make for breakfast.

A noise alerted him to her presence. He closed the refrigerator and glanced into the great room. "Hi."

Rachel stood there wearing a pair of gray and red holiday pajamas, her curls piled on top of her head and wrapped with a scarf. Her eyes widened, their golden color going molten, and her gaze flickered over him from head to toe.

She flushed becomingly. "Good morning. You look…well."

His chest bursting with gratitude, desire, and an undefined emotion he wasn't ready to acknowledge, he strode over and pulled her into an embrace. After a brief moment of tension, she melted into him, wrapping her arms around his back, all warm, soft, and lush curves. The sugared orange scent of her curls teased his nose.

"You saved my life," he murmured into her satin scarf. "Thank you. I'm thoroughly ashamed I didn't tell you this yesterday."

"You—you're welcome."

He released her and immediately missed her presence. "How about some breakfast?"

"Coffee first, please," she said, following him into the kitchen and settling on a stool at the island.

"How do you take it?" He smiled at her look of shock. "Your coffee."

Her blush deepened. "Cream and sugar."

Seconds later, he placed a mug in front of her. She wrapped both hands around it and brought it to her nose, inhaling its aroma. She pursed her lips and blew softly on the hot liquid inside before taking a tentative sip.

Blood surged in a well-trod path southward, and he swallowed thickly. She'd turned drinking her morning coffee into one of the most sensual experiences he'd ever seen. And in these pants, he wouldn't be able to hide what he'd thought of the action.

He moved until the counter hid him from the waist down.

"With everything that's happened over the past couple of days, it just occurred to me that tomorrow is Christmas Eve."

She gasped. "Oh my god, you're right. It completely slipped my mind."

"How would you be celebrating if I hadn't shown up?"

"I'd probably stuff myself with food and watch holiday movies. Before Amelia left, I had her pick up a frozen apple pie and butter pecan ice cream, my favorite dessert." She looked stricken. "That sounds pathetic, doesn't it?"

"It sounds indulgent and completely doable." He straightened. "How about scrambled eggs and toast for breakfast?"

"Yes, please."

He smiled and began grabbing the utensils he needed. "Why aren't you spending the holidays with your family?"

She shrugged. "It's just my parents and me, and they're out of the country."

"Do they usually travel during Christmas? Where do they go? New York? Hawaii?"

Her eyes opened wide, and she laughed. "If you knew my parents, you'd know how hilarious that is. They're not on vacation. They're working. My parents have spent the past two years teaching English and critical thinking to students in Cambodia with the Peace Corps."

Wow. Now he could see where Rachel got her values.

She stared down into her cup. "They were supposed to be coming home this year, but this summer they told me they were taking another assignment. In Botswana."

Her sadness was palpable. "You haven't seen your family in over two years?"

She tightened her lips and shook her head.

Joss may get on his nerves, with her overprotectiveness and her need to interfere in his life, but not seeing her for years was a choice he wasn't willing to make.

"They send me pictures." Rachel grabbed her phone and

started scrolling until she found what she'd been searching for. She turned the screen so he could see the image.

Beneath another clear blue sky, this time against a backdrop of sun-drenched green trees and a dirt road, an older white man with glasses stood with his arm draped around the shoulders of a petite black woman. Her arm was wrapped around his waist, and they were laughing while the woman pointed to something out of the frame.

He enlarged the picture. "You have your mother's eyes."

"And my dad's nose and chin. I know." A slight smile curved her lips before she placed the phone screen down on the counter.

"Was that taken in Cambodia?"

Rachel nodded.

"Your parents take their charity work very seriously," he said, impressed by people who walked the talk.

"That's how they raised me. If you want the world to be better, you have to do your part. We all have a responsibility to help those who are less fortunate."

She'd said that yesterday. That she'd *had* to help him.

He cracked several eggs in a bowl and began whisking the mixture. "That's very... unselfish of you."

She shrugged again, matter of factly.

"Is that why you're here? Your family is out of the country, so you decide to spend the holiday by yourself in a mountainside chalet?"

"Not exactly." She sighed. "Remember when you asked me if I was running away from someone?"

He did, and his chest tightened at the notion that there may be another man in her life.

"A couple of weeks ago," she continued, "I intervened in a situation outside of my apartment building."

He knew from how she phrased that sentence that there was more to the story than what she was telling. "Is that why you needed to get out of town?"

She dipped her chin and averted her gaze. "People made a bigger deal of it than was necessary. I could've stayed in DC."

He narrowed his eyes. He didn't like her evasiveness. "People?"

"The police."

He tensed. "A bigger deal of what?"

She tipped her head back and looked up at the ceiling. "I saw a woman being abused by her boyfriend on the street, and I intervened. The boyfriend wasn't too happy about it and he's, uh... kinda been...stalking...me."

His insides churned as his mind quickly calculated the number of ways that scenario could've gone wrong. His fingers curled tightly around the spatula in his hand. "Do you know how dangerous that was? You could've been killed."

"Life is dangerous. I could've been killed yesterday when I ventured out to help you. Does that mean I shouldn't have done it? Or do you believe your life is more important than hers?"

Oh, she was good, he thought admiringly. Her questions might've shut down many people who'd decline to argue further, but he knew there was a distinction between the two lines of reasoning.

"This wasn't an either/or situation," he argued. "You should always assess the danger and weigh the risks involved. Sometimes you can't interfere, no matter how much you may want to. I'm not saying my life is more important than the woman you saved, but the question you should ask is which situation was more threatening? With me, you risked the possibility of exposure. That man could've hurt or killed you."

His heart pounded mercilessly in his chest, his worry about her being in peril shaking him more than he'd expected.

"She needed help and everyone else just stood there and watched, like it was some goddamned entertainment. You didn't see the look in her eyes. You didn't see her fear. She was all alone out there. What was I supposed to do? Wait? Do nothing?"

"Yes!"

She shook her head. "I told you yesterday, I couldn't have done that. It's not how I'm wired."

She was amazing. Mere minutes before, he'd been clear about his thoughts and his opinion of how she should've handled that situation. But she'd painted such a vivid picture that he had a hard time believing he wouldn't have intervened and helped the woman himself.

He poured the beaten eggs into the heated pan. "I'm seeing a pattern emerge here. You have a habit of leaping to help others with no concern for your own safety."

She snorted. "You have no idea."

He arched a brow. "Really? I have to hear this."

She gazed up at him through lowered lashes. "I don't know. Can I trust you?"

Though he knew she was joking, his response to her was quite serious. "I hope so. Because I trust you. With my life."

"Oh," she gasped, appearing to be at a loss for words.

Okay, Jackson, you went a little too fast there. Time to lighten it back up.

He slid four slices of bread into the toaster and pressed the lever. "Your secret's safe with me. And like they say, what happens in Jackson Hole—"

"Ugh, please don't." She curled her lip and held up a hand. "I'd like to find whoever came up with that Vegas slogan and wring their necks."

He laughed. "Then spill."

The mixture began setting in the pan, so he took the spatula and gently pulled the eggs across the heated surface, forming large fluffy curds.

"When I was ten," she began, "we learned how the overcrowding of landfills worked to deplete the ozone layer. As you can imagine, I was very concerned."

"Indeed." He nodded, his lips twitching.

She shifted in her seat. "So I wrote up a report and begged my parents to take me to the next town council meeting. Either the mayor didn't understand the issue or wasn't interested in having it brought up before the council. He was completely condescending. He practically patted me on my head and pushed me out of the door."

He waited with bated breath to hear how young Rachel got her revenge.

"All I wanted was for the town to consider offering a recycling service along with the trash collection."

He turned off the burner and added the cooked eggs to both plates. "Seems very reasonable."

"I know, right? Since the straightforward approach didn't work, I resorted to Plan B."

"Which was?"

"I convinced some kids in my neighborhood to load up their wagons and bicycle baskets with plastic containers, cardboard boxes, and soda cans, and we rode over to the mayor's house and dumped it all on his lawn."

That was hardcore for a ten-year-old. "What did your parents say?" He slid a plate, a napkin, and a fork in front of her.

"My globe-trotting, service-oriented, liberal educator parents?" She stared down at her plate and smiled. "This looks incredible. Thank you. My parents were amused. They saw it as a citizen protest. The mayor did not. He called it vandalism and told me I'd better clean it up by the following afternoon if I didn't want to end up in juvie. Unfortunately, while the other kids were happy to help trash his yard, they weren't as keen to help clean it up."

He laughed. When the toast popped up, he gave her two slices and kept the other two for himself. "That story was even better than I imagined. You were like a little Norma Rae or Erin Brockovich."

She pointed her fork at him. "Change that to Little Miss Flint and we'll be good. As good as these eggs." She shook her head. "I hadn't thought about that incident in forever. It must've been five years ago when I visited my parents and one of their friends mentioned the March on Willow Ave."

He almost choked on his eggs. "It had a name?"

"Yeah." Her eyes twinkled. "The mayor lived on Willow Avenue."

The more he learned about her, the more he wanted to know. It was the same burning curiosity he'd felt when they first met. Only this time, he had no plans to leave early. "Let me guess. This social activism wasn't a onetime deal, was it?"

"Not really."

"There are more stories?"

"Possibly," she said, grinning as she took another bite of food.

"Are you going to share them?"

"Sure. One day," she said.

Jackson wondered if she was aware that her response hinted that they'd see more of each other in the future. He decided not to draw her attention to it. It allowed him to hope.

Her mouth twisted in wry amusement. "I'm glad you find these stories entertaining. They weren't the easiest for me to live through, and they definitely didn't make me the most popular girl in high school."

Rachel Williams was one of the most stunning women he'd ever seen, and teenage boys were nothing but superficial. "I find that hard to believe."

"That doesn't mean it's not true. I was a freak. Between my outspoken nature and my parents' eccentric lifestyle, boys weren't lining up to ask me out. Especially when it was known that I wasn't going to put out."

He winced. Yeah, that was the other thing about teenage boys.

"But I am who I am. I may not always handle situations in the best way, but I have good intentions. I've never regretted standing up for what I believed was right." A smile teased her lips, and she lowered her lashes. "Even when it cost me my scholarship in college."

"Oh, come on! Now you're just being mean," he said, when it

was clear she wasn't going to elaborate. He stood, took their plates and put them in the sink. "Why don't you go grab a shower, and when you come back we'll look into those holiday movies you mentioned."

The smile that broke across her face took his breath away. "I won't be long."

He rubbed the spot on his chest over his heart. "It doesn't matter. I'll be waiting."

When she returned twenty minutes later, he'd showered, cleaned the dishes, turned on the fireplace, and found the surprise Joss had mentioned.

And speaking of surprise...

Rachel had changed into a flowing red dress that clung to her lean figure and enhanced the rosiness in her skin.

"You look beautiful."

"Thank you," she said. Her eyes widened at the boxes on the counter, and she hurried over. "Christmas decorations! Where did you find them?"

"I called my sister. She mentioned they had some stored here."

The other surprise she'd included was in his pocket.

"I didn't know how much I was going to miss decorating for the holidays until I saw these." She bounced from foot to foot as she dug through the ornaments. "Let's put them up."

He rubbed his chin. "Where? We don't have a tree."

"We don't need a tree. Not when we have that gorgeous fireplace and those floor to ceiling windows!"

A wide grin brightened her beautiful face as she examined the contents in the boxes, each new reveal eliciting sounds of delight and satisfaction. He found her exuberance contagious and couldn't resist going along with her plans.

Nodding, he asked, "Shall we start with the fireplace?"

Working together, it didn't take long for them to turn the chic, rustic great room into a cozy holiday haven. They placed a pre-lit garland loaded with frosted sprigs of berries along the large wooden mantle, set various holiday ornaments and trimmings on tables and flat surfaces around the space, and added festively themed pillows and throws to the sofa and chairs.

Jackson took the lavish poinsettia-laden wreath and hung it on the front door. With frigid temperatures and a stretch of undisturbed snow that seemed to extend to the horizon, it was unlikely anyone else would see it, but Rachel had been adamant that the outside also benefit from the yuletide makeover.

Shutting out the cold, he smiled and hurried back, only to pull up short just inside the living room. Rachel had hauled a small leather ottoman over to the windows and was attempting to drape string lights onto the clear plastic hooks strategically placed along the top of the frames.

He frowned. "I thought we'd agreed I was going to do that."

"I didn't agree," she said, her tone distracted as she focused on her task. "I just didn't argue."

"Rachel—"

"I'm fine. Besides, I'm not the one with a bum knee."

She reached farther, stretching up on her toes, the slim lines of her body silhouetted by the fluid fabric of her dress.

"My knee is fine." He started across the room, anxiety churning in his stomach. "Come down and let me finish."

"Almost...done." She shifted her weight too far forward.

As if in slow motion, he saw the ottoman slide on the wooden floor.

"Rachel!"

Jackson wasn't sure what superpower he tapped into in order to channel the speed and agility necessary to traverse the room and catch her in his arms before she fell, but he made it in time.

"That was unexpected." She shook her head and swallowed, blinking slowly as she gazed up at him. "Thank you."

"You're welcome."

His heart banged against his chest and his breath caught in his throat as he stared at her. God, she was so fucking gorgeous! And he wanted to be with her. More than he'd wanted anything in a long time. He'd decided he wouldn't leave this place, leave *her*, without doing everything he could to make that happen. Blood thickened his cock, as if to emphasize the urgency of his intent.

"Um..." She caught her lush bottom lip between pearly white teeth. "You can let me up now."

"Right." He slowly straightened, ignoring the recurring ache in his knee, until they were standing so close that he thought he'd lose himself in her whiskey-colored eyes. He inhaled the spicy citrus scent he was coming to associate with her, need flooding his body.

What he was considering was preposterous, but he had to try. Although he'd been loath to admit it, the ache of their missed encounter had been tormenting him for six months. Surely she'd felt the same way?

What if she hadn't? What if she rejected him?

He wouldn't know until he asked. But first—

"Does this make us even?"

"Even?" She snorted. "That's a bit of a stretch. I saved your life. You saved me from a few bruises. I hardly think they're equal."

"Fair." He brushed aside a curl that had snagged on her lashes. "But I did prevent you from being hurt. That has to count for something, right?"

At this touch, she exhaled shakily. "Maybe."

"Good. Because I need your help with another project."

She rolled her eyes. "No fair. You know those words are my kryptonite."

He certainly hoped so. "I was thinking about our conversation yesterday. About doing better in the giving department."

"Oh?" Her expression brightened. "Of course. Do you want the names of some worthy charities that would be a good match for RRG?"

He would. Later. "You said the more I gave, the more I'd come to love giving."

"Yes," she said tentatively, her brows lowered.

Here we go... He took a deep breath. "I need you to help me by allowing me to give."

"I don't understand."

"I want to give. To you."

She frowned and jerked her head back. "I don't want your money."

He believed her. Even in their short time together, he knew she cared very little about his wealth outside of how he could use it to help others.

"I'm not offering you money. I want to give you something you might find more enjoyable. I'm offering you pleasure."

Chapter Six

Rachel gasped. Had she heard Jackson correctly? "You want to give me...*pleasure*?"

"I do," he assured her calmly, his gaze steady on hers.

In bed? Was that what he'd meant? Was this the wildest thing she'd ever heard?

Was it wrong that she was actually considering it?

What woman wouldn't? Jackson Randolph was smart, rich and sexy as hell. Just thinking of the possibilities made her heart race and heat flush her chest.

Still...

"Why?"

Grooves appeared between his brows. "What do you mean, 'why'?"

"Where is this coming from?" She swallowed, trying to clear the sudden apprehension tickling the back of her throat. "Is it... because I saved you during the snowstorm?"

He shrugged. "It was a factor."

Disappointment tinged with anger flared in her belly. She curled her lip. "While offering to fuck me to express your gratitude is certainly novel, it isn't necessary. A gift basket would suffice!"

Feeling the telling burn behind her eyelids, she turned and walked away, not wanting to give him the satisfaction of witnessing the evidence of her distress.

"Dammit, Rachel!" He grabbed her arm and spun her back to face him. "I meant that almost dying and thinking I'd never see you again had shifted my perspective and made me realize I don't want to live with regret. And I know if I don't show you how I feel, I'll always regret it. I'm not suggesting this out of some sort of misplaced gratitude. I'm doing it because you're one of the most caring and compassionate women I know. Because you're beautiful, smart, funny, and brave and the way you give your all to the causes you believe in inspires me to do better. To *be* better. But mainly I'm doing it because I want you so goddamned much I can't see straight, and I'd love nothing more than to drop to my knees and worship every single inch of your body!"

Rachel blinked, stunned by his words. Wow.

His chest rose and fell from the vehemence of his outburst, but his gaze burned into hers. And suddenly, there was no doubt in Rachel's mind about what she was going to do.

"Be selfish. Do something frivolous, strictly for your benefit... Have a fling..."

Her boss's advice rang in her mind.

Say less, Sharon.

Plus, Rachel had never been able to turn away someone who needed her help.

She trailed her fingers against his jaw. "What would that...involve?"

A flush tinged his cheekbones, and he lifted his hand to cover hers. "Whatever you want. That's kind of the point."

She licked her bottom lip. "Is this like cooking-for-me-doing-the-dishes type of pleasure or toe-curling-back-breaking-screaming-out-loud-orgasms type of pleasure?"

His nostrils flared. A slow, delicious smile eased across his face. "That's a lot of pressure, but definitely the latter."

Adrenaline coursed through her body, heightening her senses and sending her imagination into overdrive. But she needed to make sure they were on the same page. "And just to be clear: this gift of pleasure is just for today, right?"

He hesitated and Rachel tensed, from anticipation or dread, she wasn't sure. But after a few moments, he nodded.

"If that's what you want," he said, his tone light.

Not a direct answer, but close enough. Because despite her stipulation, she wanted this experience. And finally, the opportunity to finish what they'd started all those months ago. That would be enough. It had to be. They were too different. She couldn't expect anything more—like a relationship—with Jackson.

Could she?

You can think about this later. Now's the time for feeling.

Her gaze dropped to his mouth. "I loved kissing you. Can we start there?"

"Aww, baby. Absolutely."

Closing the space between them, he cupped both of her cheeks in his hands and stared into her eyes. A tiny corner of her heart melted at the fervor simmering in his gaze. He looked at her like a treasured possession he'd once lost and had been blessed to find again. Butterflies soared in her belly as she eagerly awaited what was to come.

Jackson slid his thumb across her bottom lip, then gently, sweetly, brushed her mouth with his. The contact sent a blast of tingles throughout her nerve endings, almost like an advanced warning to her erogenous zones.

Hey guys, remember this? It's gonna be good!

And hot damn, it was. His starting kisses were brief, open-mouthed, and soft. With each kiss, their lips clung when they parted as if they, too, never wanted the embrace to end. Her insides soared, and she grabbed onto his forearm, needing something to ground her, to keep her from taking flight.

When the frustration of not getting more began to claw at her, his tongue trailed along her lips, seeking entrance. She granted it with no hesitation, moaning as he finally deepened the kiss.

During their previous encounter, their kisses had rocked her world. She'd been grateful to the wall at her back and him at her front for holding her up when her knees threatened to buckle. But these kisses were even better, and she filled them with all the passion she'd kept bottled for the past six months.

And the way he kissed her?

As if her mouth, lips, and tongue gave him life.

He wanted to give her pleasure? He was doing a damn fine job of it.

"Does that feel good?" he asked, nibbling along her jaw.

She tilted her head, granting him better access. "Uh-huh."

"What else do you like?" he whispered, his voice teasing her skin.

"You want to talk about this *now*?"

He pulled back. "Can you think of a better time?"

Excellent point.

He kissed the corner of her mouth and her cheek. "What if I nibble on your ear?"

He proceeded to do just that, biting the fleshy part of her lobe, then tonguing the ridges and valleys of the sensitive organ, his tongue flicking against the inner canal.

Her pussy pulsed, and she moaned.

"Ooh, you like that, did you?" He smiled, his lips curving against her skin. "Did I tell you I love the sounds you make? When we were in that room and you were breathing heavy, and moaning... Damn baby, I almost came in my pants."

His dirty talk was seriously turning her on. She wanted to play, too. She licked her lips. "I did like it. A lot. It made my pussy wet. Wanna feel?"

He stiffened and growled low in his throat.

She ran her hands up his chest and across his shoulders. "Is that a yes?"

"That's a *hell* yes!"

Good. Because she really wanted him to touch her. The way he had that night.

Staring deep into his eyes, she lifted her dress and guided his fingers beneath the waistband of her panties. "Press in," she whispered.

His wrist flexed in her grip as he did, and her lashes fluttered closed.

"Harder."

When he complied, she trembled, bucking her hips forward.

"So fucking hot," Jackson murmured. He took control, sliding his fingers through her curls and along her inner lips. "You were right. You *are* wet."

She tossed her head back, the sensations stealing her breath. "I...don't...lie."

"Good to know."

He captured her mouth again, his fingers continuing to work their magic between her thighs. She writhed against him, both shocked and amazed at the neediness she presented.

This wasn't like her.

At all.

She hadn't dated much, being too busy for a typical social life. The few brave souls who showed interest eventually tapped out when it became clear she wasn't going to morph into a simpering arm accessory just because they shared a few kisses. Which explained why she was still a virgin when she'd graduated from high school.

College had been a different story. She'd found her tribe, and her loneliness—and her celibacy—ceased to be. But the world was a mess, people needed help, and her time was precious. She'd never found someone worth the distraction.

Until now.

"You mentioned regret. You know what I regret most?" he asked, when the necessity for air drew them apart.

The same thing she regretted now? That they hadn't been doing this for the past six months? "What?"

"That I never got to taste you."

Well, *now* she regretted *that*, too.

"May I?"

Who knew manners could be so sexy? What was it he'd said? "Hell, yes."

His smile was pure sin. He removed his fingers from her panties and stuck his index finger in his mouth.

"Hmmm. A delicious sample to tide me over."

She shivered. Was it possible to come simply from anticipation?

He led her over to the couch. Once she was seated, he dropped to his knees before her. He hooked his hands beneath her thighs and tugged her toward him until she lay flat on her back, with her feet on the floor.

She could get used to this.

He lifted the hem of her dress and settled it around her waist. When his gaze met hers again, he looked like he was ready to devour her.

He licked his lips. "I've dreamed about this for six months. Hell, I jerked off to it two nights ago. So I'm going to take my time."

The idea of Jackson stroking his cock while thinking of her caused a delicious heat to inflame her core.

He spread her thighs and the air in the room whispered over her warm flesh, causing goose bumps to rise on her skin. Starting at her knees, he ran his hands up her bare legs, sensation flaring in their wake, until his thumbs rested in the crease between her upper thigh and pelvis. He squeezed and more moisture flooded her.

He stared at her black cotton panties. Swallowed. "Let me see that pretty pink pussy. Lift your hips for me."

Oh, his words...

She did and, he pulled them leisurely—frustratingly so—over her hips and down her legs, before allowing his tongue to make the return trip; over her ankle, up her calf, behind her knee, and along her inner thigh—

Halting way too short of her goal.

She clenched the sofa cushions in her fingers. "Why did you stop?"

He chuckled, and the gentle expulsion of breath teased her sensitive flesh. "You're very demanding."

But there was no censure in his tone.

Only reverence.

"And so beautiful."

Spreading her legs wider, he leaned forward and slayed his objective to give her pleasure.

"Oh, god," she breathed. This man was a master with his fingers and tongue. He sucked, finger-fucked, and stroked all parts of her pussy until her pulse, her heartbeat, her body were in sync with the throbbing in her clit.

In the past, she hadn't always found the experience of receiving oral sex pleasurable. Guys had either stabbed painfully at her clit with their tongue, licked her with a tongue so dry it felt like they were scouring her vulva, or they'd stopped after a few minutes, expressing surprise she hadn't already come.

But Jackson did none of that. He loved her, savored her, kissed and licked parts of her she hadn't even known were sensitive. Which made sense. Because his presence, his touch, was a key ingredient to her pleasure.

It felt good. *Soooo good.* Her hips bucked, her thighs quivered, and she gripped his hair and pressed as close as she could get to his talented mouth while keening sounds of lust issued from her.

But she didn't come.

It was right there, this bright and amorphous blob of light, hovering just beyond her grasp.

Guilt worked its annoying presence into her mind. Her breathing slowed and her heartbeat slipped back to normal.

Jackson lifted his head. "Hey. Where'd you go?"

"Nowhere. I'm fine."

He pulled back. "Is everything okay? Did I do something you didn't like? Tell me and I'll fix it."

"No, you were great. But I'm good. You can stop now if you want."

He frowned. "Why would I stop?"

"I don't know."

He stroked her thigh. "You can tell me anything. You've nothing to fear from me. I won't judge you. I just want to know what's going on."

This was so embarrassing!

She squeezed her eyes shut. "Because it's taking too long," she wailed.

The resulting silence was deafening. Then—

"Rachel."

She squeezed her eyes tighter and shook her head, mortified by what she'd admitted. She may not have a lot of experience, but she didn't want to come off as some frigid ice princess.

"Baby, I'm not going anywhere. I promise. And I meant what I said. My only thought, goal, mission, is to give to you. And it'll take as long as it takes. If you don't like what I'm doing, I'll stop. But if you're enjoying it half as much as I am, then don't worry about the time. I'm in no rush. There's no place else I'd rather be."

Cautiously, she opened her eyes to face an earnest, caring expression that matched his heart-melting words.

She cupped his cheek. "Not even Portland?"

He laughed softly. "Not even Portland."

With a soft sigh, she leaned back and relaxed, allowing her thighs to fall open. Jackson dipped his head...

And many...she had no idea the exact amount...minutes later, that bright amorphous light engulfed her, and sensations narrowed to a pinpoint, before exploding in a dizzying paroxysm of pleasure.

He brought her back to earth with sweet kisses along her inner thighs and a lingering one on her mouth. She moaned, unbelievably aroused by the taste of *her* essence on *his* lips.

He palmed her. "Are you ready for more?"

She nodded. *Oh yeah.* And this time, she was going to be the one in control. She scooted into a seated position. "There is something I want. Stand up."

"Okay."

She smiled when he obeyed her order. "Now, take off your pants."

One dark brow lifted, but again, he acquiesced to her demand, revealing trim hips, strong thighs, and muscular calves.

Moisture flooded her mouth at the outline of the package straining to be free of his black boxer briefs.

She swallowed. "Take them off."

His cock sprang free—long, veined, and not too thick. Perfect. She curled her fingers around his shaft, thrilled by its velvet steeliness, and stroked him from base to tip and back again. His responding hisses were music to her ears, and her core tightened in anticipation.

She knew a lot of people took this act lightly, thought oral sex was no big deal, but she couldn't ignore the intimacy of what he'd done to her and of what she was now doing to him. The trust required, the vulnerability shared, the power.

She glanced up at him through her lashes and was thrilled to see his head flung back, his mouth slack. She wasn't particularly skilled in this arena, either, but she intended to follow her instincts.

Leaning forward, she took him in her mouth and rubbed her tongue on the underside of his cock, pushing the head to the roof of her mouth. Her eyes fluttered close as her body burst into flames. She reveled in the sensation of his cock sliding against her tongue, the sounds of titillation he made, and the smell of arousal permeating the air. The pure carnality of it invaded her, and she allowed it to take over until all she wanted was everything he had to give.

She flicked her tongue along his length until she reached his balls, drawn tight against the base of his shaft. Holding his cock high with her right hand, she flattened her tongue and swept it over the thin, soft skin of his testicles. She curled her tongue around them and gathered them into her mouth, surprised that she loved the way they felt.

"Goddamn, woman! What are you doing to me?" he growled, slipping his hands into her curls and gripping her skull.

Liquid heat pooled between her thighs, and her pussy seemed to swell. She didn't know who was enjoying this more, him or her.

She followed the seam that led her back to the head. She suckled the meaty tip, getting it nice and wet, and allowed the extra saliva to run down the shaft. Then she licked her lips, firmed them, and slowly pushed his cock into her mouth, hoping to create a warm, wet, tight seal that would mimic the feel of her pussy.

A tortuous moan rumbled from his chest, confirming she'd succeeded.

She did it again, this time increasing the vacuum suction as she pulled him out.

"Enough!" He tugged himself from her mouth and staggered back several paces.

She smeared her thumb across her lower lip. "I thought you liked what I was doing? Don't the same rules apply?"

He stood before her, his chest rising and falling, his penis erect and extended away from his body, bobbing slightly and brushing the hem of his shirt.

"They do. And if I didn't like what you were doing, I'd tell you. But that's the problem. I like it *too* much. Three more seconds and I was going to come in your mouth. Unless...do you want me to?"

She considered, then nixed the idea. She wouldn't allow

anything to get in the way of finally knowing the feel of him inside of her. No matter how enticing the proposition.

"Next time," she said. "We'll add that to the list."

He grinned. "Oh, we have a list now?"

"Uh-huh." She stood and placed her hands on his shoulders, then maneuvered him so he was the one seated and she was standing.

He stared up at her. "Interesting how you've managed to gain control of the situation."

Again, he didn't say it as if it was something negative. "Isn't it though?"

"What are you doing now?"

She dropped a knee onto the sofa. "This is our first time. I want to look at you."

A flush dotted his cheekbones. "I'm glad you said that. Because we'll be doing this again. Over and over, into the foreseeable future."

She lifted her dress over her head and straddled his hips.

"Wait," Jackson said, reaching for his pants on the floor. He pulled a condom out of his pocket.

She tilted her head. "Were you a Boy Scout?"

"I'll tell you about it later," he said, tearing open the wrapper and quickly sheathing himself.

And then it was time. The moment she'd been waiting for since they'd first met.

Rachel rose and braced trembling hands on Jackson's shoulder. He gripped her hips and, staring into each other's eyes, they both lowered her onto his long, hard length, each delicious inch abrading her in the most exquisite way.

He muttered several curses when he was buried to the hilt. "Motherfucking damn, baby..."

She rejoiced in their joining. It felt right. Is this why she and Jackson had ended up here at the same time? The reason for this massively unbelievable coincidence?

Was this meant to be?

She pressed her forehead to his and began to move as temporarily dormant sensations roused to life. The friction against her already aroused walls felt so good she wanted to scream.

She did, the sound issuing from her like a lusty exaltation, followed by a low, needy whine.

"That's it, baby. Let me know how much you like it."

"Do you like it?" she panted.

"More than like it. I love it. This pretty pussy of yours was made for me."

He palmed her breasts. They were so sensitive that when he squeezed and kneaded them, her breath caught in her throat.

"And these titties," he groaned. "They're the perfect size. Just right for my hand."

"That's what you said the last time."

"Bears repeating."

He plucked her nipples between his thumb and forefinger, then leaned forward and took one hardened bud into his mouth.

Sparks of bliss flared through her.

Rachel gripped the back of the sofa and rode him. The ethereal agony of sliding up and down his cock overwhelmed her. She wanted as much of him in her as possible and still it wasn't enough. Up and down she moved, undulating her hips in a whirlwind of ecstatic frenzy, bringing her closer and closer to the pinnacle she craved.

They kissed, and his tongue caught her moans and gasps. He grabbed her ass and shifted her pelvis forward so her clit ground against the ridge of his cock. That one move tilted her world on its axis as the rapture built again, the tension growing stronger and wilder.

"Jackson..."

"Come on, baby," he panted, his hips surging upward to slam into her. "Come for me."

"Sooo good," she keened, throwing her head back. The walls of her pussy contracted, the bright light engulfed her, and she bucked forward, crying out as pleasure briefly robbed her of all coherence.

Her climax seemed to have triggered his own. His fingers clutched her hip and he rammed into her, roaring as he joined her in oblivion.

Afterward, she curled up on his lap and rested her head on his shoulder.

"You called me Jackson. Jackson, not Jack." he murmured, his lips curving into a soft smile.

"Hmmm," she murmured, hugging him tight. "Oh, and remember what I said about the gift basket instead of fucking me? Scratch that. I still want that gift basket. Harry & David. The bountiful harvest one with the pears."

She kissed his cheek and then drifted off, feeling sated, protected and not alone for the first time in years.

Chapter Seven

"...This gift of pleasure is just for today, right?" Jackson's stomach churned at the thought, and he brushed a finger along Rachel's cheek. Being with her had been better than he'd ever imagined. And knowing no one had taken the time to give her pleasure but that she'd trusted him to do so...

His heart shifted in his chest.

What they'd done hadn't assuaged his hunger for her. If anything, it increased his appetite; made him want more. As far as he was concerned, "just for today" wasn't an option. There was no telling how much longer they would be stranded here. They needed to discuss all the ways they had at their disposal to pass the time.

What about after you leave?

The distress that stiffened his muscles rocked him to his core. He needed to ponder the depth of that reaction.

But not now. He wanted to spend more time with her in the intimacy of the detente they'd created. Gently, he gathered a sleeping Rachel up in his arms and strode toward their rooms.

She roused. "What are you doing?"

"Moving someplace more comfortable."

"But your knee—"

Damn thing twinged when she mentioned it. He shifted her. "My knee is fine."

"Jackson!" She struggled slightly. "I can walk."

"I know. But do you like that I'm carrying you?"

She flushed. *So fucking adorable.* "It's ridiculous."

Ridiculous? He'd show her ridiculous. He jostled her. "Do you like it?"

Warmth suffused him as she laughed and clutched at his shoulders.

"Yes," she shrieked.

He hugged her securely to his chest. "Then consider this me giving you pleasure."

"Okay," she said, relaxing into his hold. "To my room, if you please."

"Your room, my room, it doesn't matter. As long as we use a bed this time."

"This time?" Her brow rose. "There's more?"

"Well, you said today, and a day is technically twenty-four hours."

"I believe you're right, Mr. Randolph." She smiled widely and wound her arms around his neck. "How about a brief rest before round two?"

Christmas Day

Jackson's hand tightened around Rachel's as he escorted her across the basement to the closed door in the far corner.

"Back here?" Rachel asked.

"Uh-huh."

Turning the knob, he pushed the door open and flipped the

switch on the wall. Fluorescent light illuminated the moderately sized storage room. The space was well organized, with labeled boxes and storage containers stacked in rows of freestanding wood and metal shelving units. He stood back and motioned for Rachel to precede him. "You're certain you saw brownie mix in here?" she asked.

He'd been staring at her ass, his mouth going dry at the way the material of her leggings hugged each globe, providing maximum bounce when she walked. His palms itched, and he'd made a mental note to see if she'd be into a little playful spanking.

But at her question, his gaze flew up to find Rachel staring at him over her shoulder, a frown marring her brow.

He wiped his face of any expression. "Uh, yeah. Over there."

He pointed in the direction of the closest shelf.

She pursed her lips. He worried she was on to him, but she walked over and grabbed the gray plastic tote, placing it on the rectangular folding table. "I can't believe this room was here. Amelia forgot to mention it." She removed the container's lid and began looking through its contents.

"That's understandable," he said, coming up behind her and resting his hands on her shoulders. "She was probably in a hurry to get to her mother."

"You're right."

He allowed himself a moment to savor those two words. Who knew when Rachel would make that admission again?

However, he didn't let the momentary achievement distract him from his larger mission. He kneaded her shoulders and pressed a kiss to the spot just beneath her ear.

She stilled. "What are you doing?"

He dragged his tongue down the slim column of her neck to the junction where it met her shoulder. When he sank his teeth into that sensitive flesh, she shivered. He smiled against her skin. "If it isn't obvious, then I haven't been doing a good job over the past two days."

She spun in his arms to face him, her lovely eyes glowing.

"You've been doing an outstanding job. No one could ever question your skill or your dedication. You've given until I've hurt."

He chuckled. While watching one of her holiday movies, they'd engaged in some light petting, which had led to heavy foreplay and had ended with them fucking in front of the fireplace and Rachel with a bad case of rug burn on her knees. She'd brushed it off, laughingly saying she'd been marked.

He cupped her cheek. "I still feel horrible about that."

"I don't. It was totally worth it." She looped her arms around his neck. "In fact, I personally intend to write to Living thru Giving and tell them how much you've given to me. That should gain you *some* points. Maybe enough to drop down to number four on their list?"

Warmth surged through his body and his cock stirred. "I'd appreciate any help you can offer."

"As you know, helpful is my middle name."

"No, it's not. It's Sinclair."

When their lips met, he thought he'd readied himself for the rush of sentiment to follow.

He hadn't.

There was no way to prepare. Every mating of their mouths, each nibble on her lower lip, every sigh and moan he captured with his tongue, the same wave of rightness swept over him, confirming this was meant to be.

They'd awakened this morning like two kids excited to find a pile of gifts beneath the Christmas tree. But all he'd planned to unwrap was her. She'd made them French toast and hot chocolate and they'd sat in the great room, eating and sharing sweet kisses in front of the roaring, crackling fire. Afterwards, he'd handed her an envelope containing his present to her: a sizeable donation in her name to a domestic violence shelter in DC.

"Thank you," she'd said, placing a hand over her heart. He knew she'd value that offering more than any expensive piece of jewelry.

But the gift giving wasn't over. She'd surprised him with a

contribution she'd made to an environmental nonprofit that planted trees in DC's poorer parks and neighborhoods. A playground would get a newly designated green space, with trees and shrubbery planted... in memory of his grandfather.

Emotion had clogged the back of his throat and expanded his chest with adoration and gratitude for this incredible woman. He didn't deserve her, but he wasn't willing to give her up. Not this time.

She ended their kiss. "If we keep that up, we'll never leave this room. Let me find this mix and—"

He averted his gaze, but it was too late.

She angled her body away from him and narrowed her eyes. "There's no brownie mix, is there?"

He shook his head, unable to prevent the grin from spreading across his face.

She slapped his shoulder. "Dammit, Jackson, you got me all excited for some Christmas brownies!"

"How about I get you excited about something else?"

"You bet your sweet ass you will."

God, she was perfect.

He growled and nibbled her tender earlobe, his tongue sweeping the pulse that throbbed at the base of her neck. Her fingers sank into the hair at his nape as she arched her back, pressing her breasts into his chest. She heated his blood, sending it blasting through his veins and banishing the notion of anyone before her.

He slid a hand along her side and slipped it between her thighs, using his thumb to seek her clit through the layers of fabric.

"Are you serious?" she asked. "You want to do it in here?"

He traced a finger across her exposed collarbone. "You've been teasing me with these slouchy sweatshirts and leggings for days. And other than Joss's suite, this is the only room we haven't...experienced."

She dropped her forehead onto his chest. "Your sister will hate us."

He slipped his fingers into her curls and massaged her scalp. "I was thinking about asking her to sell me the house. After the past few days and all the memories we've made, it would be fun to come back next year."

Her back stiffened, and he could feel the tension in her posture. Slowly, she raised her head and her eyes bored into his. "Come back next year? Together?"

Granted, they hadn't discussed it, but these past few days he'd thought they were both feeling the same way.

No time like the present to find out.

He took her hands. "I thought my life would always be about RRG. That I would never want anything more than I wanted to protect my family's legacy. But you truly rescued me. Not just from the snowstorm, but from the possibility of a future without you. I know we need to spend more time together, but I don't want to lose what we've found, because I've never felt this way before. About anyone."

"Oh, Jackson." Her eyes flitted away from him, and she inhaled deeply. "I—"

The peal of a chime reverberated through the basement.

She craned her neck, trying to peer over his shoulder. "Is that the doorbell?"

"I don't care," he said, trying to claw back his frustration at the interruption. "What were you going to—"

"Jackson." The tone of her voice snatched his attention. "If someone's ringing the doorbell, that means they were able to get through."

Realization dawned.

He straightened and began searching for her pants on the floor.

"I'll find them. You go get the door," she said, shooing him away.

He pressed a quick hard kiss on her lips, then raced across the basement and took the steps two at a time, his knee protesting slightly. He hurried across the great room, barely noticing the little tabletop tree they'd hung with festive ornaments and placed on the sideboard, and threw open the front door, letting the outside world in for the first time in two days. A man wearing a neon yellow snow jacket with gray horizontal reflective strips stood on the porch.

"Just wanted to let you folks know the county finally managed to clear the road. If you have to go out, you can, but be careful of drifts as you head down."

The county finally managed—

Jackson frowned. "Don't you work for the county?"

"No. The owner of this property has a service contract with us. I'm going to clear your walkway and the driveway. The snow is pretty powdery, so it shouldn't take me long."

Jackson noted the vehicle at the base of the porch. It looked like an ATV with a snowplow blade attached to its front. If Joss agreed to sell him the house, he was definitely buying one of those.

"Thanks, and Merry Christmas."

"And a Merry Christmas to you, too." The man turned and jogged back down the steps.

Jackson closed the door and sagged back against it, raking a hand through his hair. According to Rachel, if their road had been cleared, the major ones were also passable. He could call his car service, head to the airport, and be in Portland by the end of the day.

But was that what he still wanted to do?

Rachel strode into the room, her cellphone at her ear.

"Thank you, Detective," she said. "I appreciate the call. And Crystal is okay?... Good... Yes, it's a great Christmas gift... Yes... You, too... Merry Christmas."

She caught sight of him and disconnected the call.

"Is everything all right?" he asked.

"They caught the stalker," she announced softly.

"Thank God." He gathered her into his arms, kissing the curls on top of her head. "The roads are clear."

She pressed herself tight to him. "I figured. Now you can go to Portland. And I can go home."

Why did the finality of that statement hit him like a sucker punch to the gut?

He had duties and responsibilities. So did she. But he knew what he wanted to do. He wanted to stay here with her and continue to pretend they were the only two people in the world. Except—

He wanted to build a real relationship with her more. "You never responded to what I said."

She pulled out of his embrace and dipped her head. "Don't worry. I know you probably got caught up in the moment."

Her response, unexpected and disappointing, fell upon him like a weighted blanket. Had he got it wrong? Did she not feel the same way? He grabbed on to the one thing of which he was certain.

"Don't tell me how I feel," he said.

"Fine. Then I'll tell you how *I* feel. It would never work."

"Why not? We're intelligent and capable people. If we put our minds to it, and we want it enough, we can make it happen."

She crossed her arms over her chest. "We're too different and we don't have the same vision for our futures."

"Do you still feel that way? After the time we've spent here together, getting to know one another? Loving one another?"

"Admit it: if some stroke of coincidence hadn't stranded us together here, you never would've reached out to me."

That's probably what he'd been telling himself. That she was too idealistic, too complicated, and required too much of his time and attention. Time and attention that was better spent on RRG. But he knew now that wasn't true. He would've contacted her. Because in all the time that had followed, he hadn't been able to get her off his mind.

But he could tell by the stubborn set of her jaw and tilt to her head that he wouldn't convince her of that. At least not at this moment.

As much as it pained him, he needed to let her go.

For now.

But this wouldn't be the last time they had this conversation.

He shoved his clenched fists into his pockets. "You're heading home?"

"Eventually. I signed up to volunteer tomorrow morning at the *After the Holidays* toy drive with one of the local charities here in town."

"I can send my plane back for you. I'll need to be in Portland for at least a week."

"Thank you," she said, her eyes widening. "That's kind of you."

"Who says a leopard can't change his spots? You've turned me into a giver." Conceding to the urge, he pressed a kiss to her forehead. Then, summoning all his willpower, he stepped away. "I'm going to make some phone calls. And pack."

After speaking with his pilot, driver, and several members of his executive team, Jackson grabbed his leather duffel from the closet and placed it on the bed.

This wasn't how he wanted to leave.

It wasn't an exaggeration to say the past few days had been amazing, and he knew he hadn't imagined the growing feelings between them. The glances, the touches, the kisses. The whispered words. The way they'd made love. That had all been real.

He zipped up his toiletry bag and laid it next to his folded shirts. Rachel probably needed more time. They'd moved pretty fast considering that five days ago he'd thought he'd never see her again. Now he couldn't imagine his life without her.

And she hadn't had the benefit of a near death experience.

If he could've stayed another week, he knew she'd agree that they belonged together. But while more time would be helpful for their relationship, it would be detrimental to his business. The storm had ruined his chance to get to Portland before the holidays and the mayor was heading to Hawaii with his family on the twenty-eighth. It was Jackson's last chance to convince the mayor and city manager not to withdraw their support for the RRG retail development deal.

Pleading his case with Rachel would have to wait.

But only temporarily. Because as important as RRG was, he'd come to realize it wasn't everything.

In addition to his feelings for Rachel, he'd discovered that he liked who he was with her; the other perspectives she inspired him to consider, the sides of his personality she unmasked. He wouldn't abandon those parts of himself no matter what happened between them.

He shook his head. *Stay positive, Randolph. You're not giving up. This isn't goodbye. More like, until next time.*

When he heard the doorbell, he exhaled audibly and glanced up at the ceiling. It was time. Taking a deep breath, he grabbed his bag and left his room. Rachel was waiting in the foyer and his heart shifted in his chest. There was so much he wanted to say to her.

Don't give up on us!
We can be great together!
I'll talk to you soon!

He settled for, "I guess this is it. Merry Christmas, Rachel."

And he couldn't even look her in the eye when he said it.

Before she could respond—and before the sound of her voice could compel him to try to plead his case once more—he ripped open the door, stepped out on the porch, and surveyed the cleared, *empty*, driveway.

He hurried back inside. "I thought the driver was here."

Rachel stood where he'd left her, hands clasped, slowly twisting back and forth. "He was. I sent him away."

"Why?"

"Your driver informed me that after he was to drop you off at the airport, he was then supposed to be on standby for me. That you'd hired him for the next few days."

He frowned. "Yes. Joss keeps a car here but driving in this weather when you're not accustomed to it...I wanted to keep you safe."

The corners of her mouth twitched. "I know. And that got me thinking..."

Hope, dizzying but tentative, bloomed in his chest.

Rachel continued. "A man who cared so much about his grandfather's legacy that he made it his life's mission to restore it, a man who donated money and resources to local causes without alerting the media even when he was shamed for being a grinch, and a man who diligently worked to give me one of the best orgasms of my life despite how long it took... that's a man worth getting to know better."

He raised a brow. "Are you saying what I think you're saying?"

"If you think I'm saying I don't want this to end and I'd love to see you when we get back to DC, then yes."

Relief nearly felled him where he stood. Dropping his bag at his feet, he crossed the space in two large strides and scooped her up into his arms. He held her tightly, unable to believe the ending he'd hoped for was actually happening.

How long they stood there, he didn't know. Eventually, he smoothed her hair back from her face and said, "I really need to go."

"I know." Her voice was muffled against his chest. "And your driver isn't gone. I told him you needed more time and sent him to the neighboring resort. He's having a late lunch on me. You're supposed to call him when you're ready."

So they had time? Perfect. A thought appeared, crystalline and fully formed, in his mind.

"Will you come with me?"

She stared up at him. "What?"

"Come with me to Portland. And then we can spend the rest of the holiday together."

She blinked. "I—I can't. I'm volunteering tomorrow, remember?"

"We can do both. I'll go with you to the toy drive in the morning and afterward we can fly to Portland."

"Will that work?"

"We'll make it work."

She sighed and gazed at him, her expression soft, eyes bright. "Is it always that easy in your world?"

He cupped her face. "It's not my world that makes it easy. It's *you* in my world. I meant what I said about not living my life without you. As long as you feel the same way, we can overcome any obstacle. We balance each other and that can only be a good thing."

Rachel turned her head to nuzzle his palm. "I'm so sorry, Jackson. I got scared. I've given to others my entire life. I didn't know any other way. And I thought that meant I was supposed to be with a certain type of person. One who committed his life to helping those in need, like my parents. I never imagined that person would come in the package of a sexy, smart ass billionaire businessman who challenged my views and taught me that being selfish isn't always a bad thing. You've shown me that it's okay to accept, to receive all the wonderful things this world has to offer. And I'm so ready to do that. Because the world gave me you."

His heart banged against his chest, as if to break free and join hers.

"I want you so much," he rasped.

A tremor rocked her body. "Then take me."

He did as she commanded, capturing her lips, delving into her mouth, taking everything she offered. Her breathing was ragged, her body hot to his touch, proof that she felt it, too.

He yanked her leggings down and resumed his interrupted journey, sliding his hands between her thighs, savoring the smoothness of her skin, until he reached the barrier of her panties. Shifting the fabric aside, he teased her folds, his pulse sprinting at her whimpers of pleasure. She moaned and arched into his touch.

"You're so wet," he said.

"Always your fault," she gasped.

His cock hardened, growing thick and heavy. He took her mouth again, their tongues dueling while he circled the sensitized nub of her clit.

She tilted her chin up and pushed her hips forward, grinding her pussy against his palm. "I'm coming!"

He stared at her, captivated by the slight flush marking her dewy skin and the moue shaping her lips. She writhed against him, her fingers digging into his shoulders, her chest rising and falling with the exertion of her pleasure, and he knew he couldn't wait a moment longer to be with her. He lifted her and moved until she was braced with her back against the wall. When she wrapped her legs around his waist, he freed himself from his pants and surged into her. They kissed, a long, slow, sweet caress that filled his soul and cemented their intention to move forward together.

Later, Rachel twined her fingers with his. "I came here because I needed a safe place to stay. But I've never felt safer than when I am in your arms." She straightened. "That reminds me. I have to call Sharon and tell her about the stalker. And us. She's never going to believe this happened."

Remembering what Joss had said about Rachel's boss, he smiled. "Somehow, baby, I think she will."

Epilogue

One year later...

District Dish
Your spot for the juicy goings on in the nation's capital...

From Grinch to Goody-Goody!

Sometimes when people are wrong, you have to call them out, and it's great when they end up the better for it. Take Jackson Randolph. Last year he was shamed by a business website on his company's poor record of charitable contributions. Since then, Rand Realty Group, the country's foremost developer of luxury shopping malls, has turned over a new leaf.

So has the gorgeous billionaire.

Many in his inner circle attribute his transformation to the stunning woman on his arm. Rachel Williams is the CEO of the newly formed Randolph Endowment, the philanthropic division of his company. Sources close to the private couple confirm they've been dating for a year, and we've got a hunch a wedding is in their future. The smitten businessman was seen visiting the workshop of DC's premier bridal jeweler just before Christmas.

Jackson Randolph is proof that you never know what you'll get when you give. So give *us* some love by subscribing and sharing our posts.

Happy Holidays, dear readers! We'll see you in the New Year!

Thank you for reading *Have Yourself a Billionaire for Christmas*. If you enjoyed it, I would love for you to leave a review. Readers appreciate hearing what other readers have to say about a book and I would be grateful for any words you'd be willing to share.

Want to stay up to date with me, access free stories from amazing authors and participate in fun giveaways? Join my monthly newsletter and receive a FREE short story.

HAVE YOURSELF A BILLIONAIRE FOR CHRISTMAS

About the Author

Tracey Livesay's latest release, **THE DUCHESS EFFECT**, is the sequel to the summer of 2022's hit book *American Royalty*, which evokes the real-life romance between Prince Harry and Duchess Meghan Markle, if Meghan was Megan Thee Stallion and was on virtually every summer 2022 reading list. Entertainment Weekly called *American Royalty* one of the "crowning achievements of the summer," The Washington Post hinted that it felt like a real-life royal romance "but steamier," and Oprah Daily praised the book as "sexy, resonant, and real." In addition to being named to *USA Today*'s list of "100 Black Novelists You Should Read," Tracey has been featured in *The New York Times, The Washington Post,* and *Entertainment Weekly,* and her book *Like Lovers Do* was named one of the 100 Best Fiction Books of 2020 by Kirkus Reviews. A former criminal defense attorney, she lives in Virginia with her husband—who she met on the very first day of law school—and is counting down the days until they have an empty nest. (Don't worry, their three kids are well aware.)

Also by Tracey Livesay

The Tycoon's Socialite Bride

Pretending With the Playboy

Love On My Mind

Along Came Love

Love Will Always Remember

Sweet Talkin' Lover

Like Lovers Do

American Royalty

The Duchess Effect

Acknowledgments

My first selfpubbed novella! It truly took a village, and many years, to bring this to fruition.

When a couple of authors approached me to be a part of a forced proximity holiday anthology back in 2017, I was stoked. It meant a lot to me that my peers thought enough of my work to include me. But 2017 was a tough year. Between finishing one of my tradpubbed books and health issues with my children, I had a difficult time getting into the story. I turned in the novella, but it wasn't my best.

Fast forward six years and four books. I hired a great editor, my writing has gotten better, and I had time... lots of glorious time, to give Rachel and Jackson the story they deserved. I hope you enjoy the sparks that fly when these two opposites get snowed in together.

My utmost gratitude and appreciation go to:

Adriana Anders, who invited me to participate in the original anthology and literally talked me back from a breakdown when things were at their most heightened;

Sarah MacLean, who "advised" me to get off my ass and republish this novella;

Rochelle French, my very first editor, I'm honored to still have her in my life and grateful that I can call on her when I need her. This story is so much stronger because of her notes and suggestions;

Mia Sosa and Adriana Herrera, for all of their encouragement and notes after reading through the finished story;

Natasha Snow, for this beautiful cover and Victoria Colotta, VMC Art & Design, for her stunning graphics;

Jannie, my assistant, whose work allows me to write in peace;

And finally, my family, who give me a real world I'm always happy to come back to.

Until the next one,
TL

American Royalty - Excerpt

In this dangerously sexy rom-com that evokes the real life romance between Prince Harry and Duchess Meghan Markle, if Meghan was Megan Thee Stallion, a prince who wants to live out of the spotlight falls for a daring American rapper who turns his life, and the palace, upside down.

Sexy, driven rapper Danielle "Duchess" Nelson is on the verge of signing a deal that'll make her one of the richest women in hip hop. More importantly, it'll grant her control over her life, something she's craved for years. But an incident with a rising pop star has gone viral, unfairly putting her deal in jeopardy. Concerned about her image, she's instructed to work on generating some positive publicity... or else.

A brilliant professor and reclusive royal, Prince Jameson prefers life out of the spotlight, only leaving his ivory tower to attend weddings or funerals. But with the Queen's children involved in one scandal after another, and Parliament questioning the viability of the monarchy, the Queen is desperate. In a quest for good press, she puts Jameson in charge of a tribute concert in her late husband's honor. Out of his depth, and resentful of being called to service, he takes the advice of a student. After all, what's more appropriate for a royal concert than a performer named "Duchess"?

Too late, Jameson discovers the American rapper is popular, sexy, raunchy and not what the Queen wanted, although he's having an entirely different reaction. Dani knows this is the good exposure she needs to cement her deal and it doesn't hurt that the royal running things is fine as hell. Thrown together, they give in to the explosive attraction flaring between them. But as the glare of the limelight intensifies and outside forces try to interfere, will the Prince and Duchess be a fairy tale romance for the ages or a disaster of palatial proportions?

Chapter One

"Duchess is here! Bitches better bow down!

D to the A to the N I / You wanna know why/ Dudes go sky high / When I say jump?/ I have no need to lie/ Open up your eyes/ The lush between my thighs/ Dudes wanna pump"
—Duchess, "Sky High"

Virginia Beach, Virginia

Sitting forward in the red leather club chair, Dani braced her elbows on her knees and bobbed her head, lip-syncing in time to the playback booming through the large airport hangar. The nasty drumbeat and thumping bass—courtesy of famed hip-hop producer SuzyQ—flowed through her, transforming her from Danielle Nelson, the tenacious young woman who'd survived being bounced from one relative's house to the next, unwanted and unappreciated, into Duchess, one of the fastest rising female rappers in the game, who'd snatch your balls before she'd let you touch her heart.

That's all they see of me
My femininity

> They think they have the key
> Silly little guy

She stood and tossed her honey-blond curls, staring down the camera on the movable crane several feet away from her, swaying her hips, seducing the lens, looking beyond the equipment through to all of the guys who'd soon be watching her.

Wanting her.

Eventually downloading the song because it was the closest they'd ever get to her.

She'd recorded her close-ups of this verse earlier today, full of sass and sex, giving them her signature head tilt and arched brow. But this part of the performance was about her movements and her body, clad to perfection in the stunning silver sequined Alberta Ferretti pantsuit the designer had lent her from the upcoming Limited Edition Fall Couture line. Dani channeled all of that charisma and raw sex appeal and felt her success in the sudden thickness of the atmosphere around her, the telltale prickle against her skin that told her she was the sole focus of everyone's attention.

> You could never see
> What I'm meant to be
> I belong to me
> D to the A to the N I

She knew what she was supposed to do as the bars to the verse ended, but she refused to execute that choreography. Instead, she freestyled some moves and struck a standing power pose.

"Cut! Going again," the assistant director called out.

The music stopped and, as if roused from stasis, people in the darkened background continued on with their tasks. The dolly grip pulled the main camera operator off to the side while the cameramen bordering the set hefted the heavy equipment off their shoulders. Someone wearing a headset handed her a bottle of water as hair and makeup swarmed, patting her face with more setting powder and taming any loose curls that dared to fight the bobby pins and extrahold hair spray.

"That was fire, Duchess," Amal said, clasping his hands together. The in-demand video director appeared from the surrounding shadows and stepped onto the set, which was decorated like a luxurious home office in a mansion.

"Thanks. It felt good," she said, handing the water back to a passing PA and waving off the beauty technicians.

"You looked strong, regal. Powerful. Buuuuut," he said, drawing the one syllable out like taffy, "what happened at the end?"

Here it comes...

She wasn't going to make it easy for him. She widened her eyes, feigning innocence. "What do you mean?"

He pointed to the pile of dollar bills heaped on the Aubusson rug. "You were supposed to tumble down to the ground and roll in the money, rub it all over your face and body. The point was to temper your strength with your femininity but make it gritty. Raw, y'know?"

It would have been one thing if she'd fucked up or he'd wanted additional coverage for the scene. But he'd loved what she'd done while on her feet; he was just pissed he hadn't forced her on her knees.

Dani closed her eyes and pictured herself in a Missy Elliott–type video where she grew several feet, her head swelled like a hot-air balloon, and she chomped down, biting the director's head clean off his body.

How's that for temper, bitch?

But when she lifted her dramatic false lashes, Amal was still standing there—head intact—smugly licking his lips, rubbing his hands together, and waiting for Dani to acquiesce to his demands.

The point was to temper your strength with your femininity but make it gritty. Raw, y'know?

Dani did know. She'd heard some version of that asinine

reasoning numerous times over the past ten years. Each time she was asked to twerk while wearing a gold string bikini, pose suggestively and touch herself while half naked, or wrap her body around a pole like a member of an X-rated Cirque du Soleil troupe.

However, the real reason she didn't want to go down on all fours for this video was because she was tired of having her image dictated by men. She wasn't ashamed of her sexuality; it was a part of her, and she owned it. But she was also aware that she viewed it differently than the men who controlled her career and dominated the industry did.

Unwilling to simply comply, she wrapped her arms around her waist, cocked her head to the side, and allowed her curls to tumble over her shoulder and rest against the brown skin of her cleavage. Amal's dark eyes followed where she led, his Adam's apple bobbing.

God! Why were men allowed to rule the world? They *thought* they were powerful, but it didn't take much to redirect the blood flow from their brains to their dicks. Even now, without uttering a single word, she'd caused beads of sweat to form on Amal's upper lip as he stared at her. He'd do anything she asked him to do.

And wasn't that true power?

You keep telling yourself that.

Because they both knew Amal was going to get what he wanted. There was a time and an occasion for confrontation and this wasn't it. As long as Dani's future—and success—was tied to the music industry, she had to play the game. And Amal was too famous for her to consider burning that bridge.

Dani thought back to the time just after her grandmother had died. For as long as she could remember, it had been her and Nana; Dani didn't know her father and barely remembered her mother. Nana had raised her with a loving, firm hand until a stroke had taken her life. Dani had been devastated and terrified. She'd felt like a small tree violently uprooted by tornado-force winds from the only forest she'd ever known. What would happen to her? Where would she go? Family had stepped in, vowing to keep her out of the system. But that claim, pledged out of love and generosity, quickly deteriorated into resentment and obligation.

It was while staying at her fourth home that year—with her mother's third cousin, Little Jessie, his wife, and their two kids—that she'd seen Eve on BET. The lyrical powerhouse had been imposing, dynamic, and everything fourteen-year-old Dani had yearned to be. She'd been certain that if she could command respect and attention like the rapper, she could finally live her life on her terms.

No more couch surfing with unenthusiastic relatives, having no say in where she landed next.

No more busting her ass doing their menial chores to "earn her keep."

No more fending off inappropriate quid pro quo sexual advances from distant male kin who should know—and do—better.

Though it hadn't seemed like it at the time, young Dani had had more autonomy over her situation than grown-ass Dani did now.

Wasn't *that* a bitch?

"So, we're going to do it again and this time you're going to stop, drop, and roll, right?" Amal crossed his arms over his fashionably ripped T-shirt.

Annoyance heated Dani's blood but she knew better than to let her irritation show on her face. "Yeah."

He tilted his chin up and stared at her down the line of his nose in that cocky, arrogant way she hated. "That's my girl."

The fuck she was.

Still, even as Dani mouthed the lyrics, rubbed the bills over her body, and made love to the camera, she forced herself to keep her inner eye on the real prize. It wouldn't be long before her fortunes would be defined by *her* decisions, and she wouldn't need to placate Amal; her manager, Cash; or any other men of their ilk. Three years ago, she'd debuted Mela-Skin, a skin-care line created for and geared specifically toward women of color. Everyone she'd initially approached to invest had rejected her, claiming she was developing an entire product line for a niche market. Roughly seventy million women were a "niche market"? The lack of respect and their inability to "see" her prompted her to do it on her own.

To everyone's surprise but hers, it was an immediate success. A year ago, a small cosmetics company had approached her about bringing the line into their portfolio. They'd wanted to buy her out completely, leaving her no say in the future of the brand, so she'd declined the offer. But it had gotten her to thinking. Running her business, not becoming a famous rapper, might be the real path to the power and autonomy she sought. And if one company had seen potential in what she'd built, wouldn't others? Upcoming meetings scheduled with the top four cosmetics and beauty companies in the world suggested the answer was yes.

The music playback ended and the assistant director yelled, "Cut!"

Amal approached her, pink tinging his golden brown skin. "Now that's what I'm talkin' bout! That was sexy as fuck! Go on. I'll see you back here in a bit."

He motioned to the AD, who added, "Moving on! Setting up the club scene."

Dani nodded her thanks, her pleasant expression collapsing as she turned away. Trying not to trip over the thick cables and lines running along the concrete floors, she headed to meet her assistant, who handed her a mason jar filled with her favorite iced vanilla coffee.

"Bless you," Dani said, taking a sip of the sweet nectar.

Tasha's lip quirked and she adjusted the black square frames on her face. "Figured you'd need it."

"You figured right. Now, as much as I love how these shoes look," she said, lifting one foot clad in a red four-inch Sergio Rossi Godiva Steel pump, "I need to get out of them."

"I got you. In four. Three. Two—" Tasha broke off as a white golf cart driven by a large black man came to a stop in front of them.

Dani grinned. She'd met her bodyguard, Antoine, when he'd been providing security for an event she attended. He'd impressed her with his top-notch skill and quiet confidence. Since celebrities were some of the most photographed people in the world, bodyguards were often caught in the frame and a lot of them started caring more about themselves and less about the people they were supposed to keep safe. But in the four years Antoine had worked for her, he hadn't shown any tendency toward that inclination. He protected her person and her privacy.

Dani settled next to Antoine. "Hey, Big Man. What's good?"

"You, lil' ma," he boomed in his deep voice. "You *wearing* that suit!"

Dani laughed and squeezed his shoulder as he maneuvered the small vehicle out of the hangar and along the parking lot, past tables filled with food, and the hair, makeup, production, and wardrobe trailers. With so many people milling around, it resembled a small town instead of a video shoot.

Dani braced an arm on the back of her seat and asked her assistant, "Did we hear from Estée Lauder?"

"Earlier today. They confirmed the meeting for next month. They just need to know if you'd prefer the New York or L.A. office," Tasha called over her shoulder from her rear-facing vantage point.

Dani nodded, excitement fluttering in her belly. Make that the top *five* companies.

"I just want the meeting. I don't care where we do it. As Janet said, 'Any time, any place,'" she sang.

"I'll check your schedule and see where you'll be then." Tasha shook her head. "You really should sing more on your albums. You have a great voice."

"Truth," Antoine said, pulling up in front of Dani's trailer.

If things went according to plan, there wouldn't be any more albums. But she was keeping that information to herself.

"You both have to say that. I pay you," Dani said, getting out of the cart.

She climbed the steps and entered her temporary home on set, the hardwood floors, dark cabinetry, and light granite surfaces screaming anonymous luxury. The bright smell of citrus essential oils was the only nod to personalization. She didn't even allow her eyes a moment to adjust to the cool, darkened interior before she slipped off the gorgeous but torturous pumps and sank down on the leather couch, moaning as she massaged the pad of her right foot.

"Up. Up. Up!" Zoe appeared from behind the door that led to the bedroom, her expression molten with horror. "You do not *lounge* in Alberta Ferretti!"

Dammit! Dani stood and quickly shed the suit, handing it to her stylist in exchange for a silk robe, which she wrapped around herself before sinking back onto the sofa. She patted her hair. "Can I take this wig off?"

"Sure. Miss K only spent an hour getting it to lay right and making your baby hairs look natural. I'm sure he won't mind doing it again."

So that was a no.

Dani frowned. "Your sarcasm isn't attractive."

"Says you."

She leaned her head gingerly on the cushion. "Do you know how much time I have before the last scene?"

"They called and told us they needed you back on set in two hours," Zoe said, zippering the pieces back into a garment bag and disappearing into the bedroom.

Which meant she had thirty minutes to relax. Maybe. She needed to contact Mela-Skin's marketing director to discuss arranging a photo shoot for their new revitalizing face mist. She also wanted to scope out the feeds of her favorite beauty influencers, see what kind of products and posts were getting the most engagement. Which reminded her . . . She hadn't checked her own social media accounts all day! She had sixty-four million Instagram followers who would be waiting to hear from her. She should go live and tease the upcoming video release; have Tasha post a few pics from the set.

The door opened and "speak of" bounded in.

"Do you have my phone?" Dani asked, not bothering to bleach the impatience from her tone.

Time was limited and her feet were still throbbing. The gladiator stilettos she was supposed to wear next wouldn't help their condition at all. But she wouldn't complain. She'd suck it up and perform her ass off.

Like she always did.

Instead of answering, Tasha responded, "It made the blogs."

Dani's head shot up so quickly she was relieved she didn't give herself a concussion. Had news of her meetings leaked?

While there was an obvious bidding war strategy to everyone being aware of all parties involved, she didn't want the companies to know she was playing them off one another this early in the game. Nothing could affect contract terms and concessions quicker than an executive's hurt feelings at learning they weren't "the only one."

She'd learned that lesson the hard way on her first album.

"Which one leaked? Coty? Genesis? L'Oréal?" She'd barely gotten the words out through gritted teeth.

"Samantha Banks."

"Samantha Banks? What does she know?"

"No. She gave TMZ a story about that incident at the club and it's trending on Twitter."

Relief slumped Dani's posture, causing her to sag back before aggravation restiffened her spine. "Can't that bitch find another coattail to ride?"

She immediately regretted her outburst. Not the sentiment—never that!—but the fact that she'd permitted Samantha Banks, of all people, to generate that amount of emotion in her.

The pop sensation with the neon-colored hair had burst onto the scene two years ago with a catchy dance tune that had become the song of the summer. Everyone, including Dani, had eagerly anticipated her follow-up . . . and they were still waiting. Banks had released several remixes of her hit, featuring famous DJs, but no new original music. That hadn't stopped her from trying to remain relevant, showing up anywhere someone even thought to erect a step and repeat.

At the VMAs last year, when Dani had accepted the award for Best Hip Hop Video for "Who You Gon' Tell," the camera had cut to the audience for reaction shots and caught Banks rolling her eyes. The press had latched onto the incident, and for weeks, they'd speculated on the tenor of Dani and Banks's relationship. Since she'd received word from Banks's camp that the singer had been reacting to the person next to her, Dani hadn't taken offense. So, she'd been stunned when the other woman had gone to Twitter to discuss their "feud."

Whenever questions arose about the existence of new Samantha Banks music, she resuscitated her "feud" with Dani. In private, Dani had no problems making her feelings known—"If she spent as much time working on new music as she did stalking me, she'd have a fucking Grammy Award–winning album!"—but she refused to comment publicly on the situation. As Nana used to say, the dog may bark at the moon, but when the moon barks back, the dog becomes important.

Dani would've felt sorry for Banks. Fame was addictive; invitations to the best parties, loads of free goodies, people knowing your name and singing your songs. It was difficult to experience the consuming phenomenon and then slide back into anonymity. But Dani hadn't been resting on *her* laurels. In addition to Mela-Skin, she'd dropped a new album and her third song from it, "Sky High," had reached number one, hence the video.

Dani hadn't worked her ass off to make Samantha Banks famous.

"Let me see," Dani said now, holding out her hand for Tasha's phone.

The TMZ headline read, "Duchess's Rebuke of Samantha Banks Has the Pop Star's Fans Calling for Her Head!"

Wait, what?

Dani knew the incident they were probably referencing. She'd been hosting a party at a club in New York last weekend and Banks had made her way to her VIP area. Antoine hadn't let her in, so she'd proceeded to insult Dani and make a scene.

"How desperate is she? No one picked up the story, so she sends a video to TMZ? Nothing about what happened will make her look good."

Dani clicked the video link embedded beneath the headline. The footage was grainy, the bouncing camera was nausea inducing, and the weird vantage point meant Dani spent the first twenty seconds looking at everyone's crotch.

Is she recording this from her purse?

The music was loud but the singer's interaction with Antoine was clear.

You can't be here, he said, calmly and professionally.

It's a free country. The retort was peevish and juvenile.

True. So, feel free to go stand someplace else.

Samantha's plaintive voice offscreen: *Look, Duchess promised to appear on my track and now her people aren't returning my calls. My fans are waiting for my new music. I just want to know if she's still going to do it.*

A hard cut to Dani, leaning over the railing yelling, *Are you serious? You gonna come up in here and say that shit to me? You're a fucking clown. Get the hell outta here.*

Antoine took Samantha's arm. *It's time for you to go!*

The video ended abruptly.

Dani turned wide eyes to Tasha. "What. The fuck. Was that?"

"Banks's new attempt to capitalize off your fame?"

"That's not what happened. When Antoine told her to leave, she basically assaulted him trying to get at me in the section. She started yelling that I was talentless and that the only reason I'd made it was because I'd spread my legs for all of the big producers in hip-hop. Security had to escort her out!"

Tasha bit her lip. "Unfortunately, she came out with the story first. And it's gaining traction."

"I wasn't aware that I was in a race to release trash takes on my career."

Tasha took the phone, swiped her thumb over the screen, and handed it back. "*Bossip* had a better take. They got your back."

Dani enjoyed *Bossip*'s clever headlines . . . when they weren't about her.

"*Duchess, You in Danger, Girl! Is Rainbow Brite Pop Star Going Single White Female on Rap Royalty with Doctored Documentary?*"

At least everyone wasn't drinking the Kool-Aid.

"You want to do a post addressing it on your Insta?"

Dani pursed her lips. "No. That would just be giving her the attention she wants."

"Are you sure?"

"Yeah. The only people who gain by me responding are Banks and the press. And since it won't put coins in my pocket, I'm not gonna participate."

Dani looked at the picture of Banks. "You tried it, little girl."

She wasn't about to let some wannabe dictate her actions. There was only one Dani "Duchess" Nelson.

And when she vacated her throne, it'd be on her terms.

Want more? Purchase your copy of AMERICAN ROYALTY now where all print and digital books are sold!

Printed in the USA
CPSIA information can be obtained
at www.ICGtesting.com
LVHW041139291123
765267LV00026B/372